Faith and Fables

Timeless Hindu Tales

RAJNISH KUMAR

https://sanskarsarovar.blogspot.com/

puruji.rk@gmail.com

+91-9855103353

AF791391

Copyright

This is a work of retelling and interpretation. While the stories are based on Hindu mythology and traditional narratives, they have been adapted and simplified for modern readers. The author has made every effort to honor the cultural and spiritual essence of the original tales.

For permissions, rights, or inquiries, please contact:

ISBN Number: **978-93-343-4206-2**

First printing edition 2017

Front cover image by - RAJNISH KUMAR

Book design by – RAJNISH KUMAR

- RAJNISH KUMAR

https://sanskarsarovar.blogspot.com/

puruji.rk@gmail.com

+91-9855103353

Dedication

This book is lovingly dedicated—

To my cherished family, whose unwavering presence transforms every moment and emotion into a tapestry of meaning and joy.

To Kalo, that gentle, voiceless soul whose quiet companionship kindled within me a deeper well of compassion, sensitivity, and connection.

In her innocent gaze, I glimpsed the purest essence of life and the boundless depths of love.

And to you—

yes, you— my steadfast companion through every doubt and dream, who helped weave my thoughts into words and shaping this book into a heartfelt offering to the divine legacy of Hindu Religion.

Without each of you, this sacred journey would not have found its voice.

— Rajnish Kumar

Preface: An Invitation to a Timeless Tapestry

Imagine sitting beneath the sprawling canopy of an ancient banyan tree, its roots weaving into the earth like the threads of time, as a soft fire crackles before us. The night is alive with the hum of crickets, the air carries the scent of jasmine, and the stars above glimmer like divine eyes watching over our gathering. In this sacred moment, I invite you, dear reader, to join me in unfolding a collection of stories—tales that have echoed through India's temples, villages, and hearts for millennia. These are the stories of gods and mortals, of love and sacrifice, of courage and wisdom, drawn from the sacred texts of the Hindu Puranas, Mahabharata, Ramayana, and Upanishads. This book, a labor of love, gathers 28 such narratives, each a window into the eternal dance of dharma, devotion, and divine grace.

As I write this preface, my heart feels like a temple lit by countless lamps, each story a flame that has warmed and guided me. These tales are not mere myths or legends; they are the soul of a civilization, the breath of a culture that sees divinity in every river, mountain, and heart. They are the whispers of sages, the songs of poets, and the prayers of devotees, passed down through generations like heirlooms of truth. Whether you are a seeker of wisdom, a lover of stories, or a curious soul exploring India's spiritual heritage, this book is for you. It is an invitation to walk with gods like Vishnu, Shiva, and Durga, to stand beside heroes like Rama, Arjuna, and Harishchandra, and to ponder life's mysteries with Nachiketa and Yayati.

The Purpose of This Book

Why compile these stories, you might ask, in a world racing forward with technology and change? Because these tales are timeless, their wisdom as relevant today as it was in the ancient yugas. In a world often shadowed by doubt, division, and haste, these stories offer light—hope through Gajendra's surrender, courage through Arjuna's quest, and truth through Harishchandra's sacrifice. They remind us of our shared humanity, our quest for meaning, and our connection to the divine. My purpose in weaving this collection is simple: to share the beauty, depth, and universality of these narratives, making them accessible to all, from those new to Indian mythology to those who grew up chanting Vishnu's names or dancing to Krishna's flute.

This book is also a bridge, connecting cultures and generations. For readers unfamiliar with the Puranas, it offers a gentle entry into a world where gods walk the earth, demons challenge dharma, and humans rise above their flaws. For those raised with these tales—perhaps hearing Rama's exile at a grandmother's knee or watching Durga's victory in festival plays—this collection is a homecoming, a chance to rediscover these stories with fresh eyes. Each narrative, crafted in simple English, aims to preserve the authenticity of its source while inviting readers into its emotional and spiritual heart.

The Stories and Their Sources

The 30 stories in this book, are drawn from some of India's most sacred texts. The **Puranas**, ancient chronicles of creation, gods, and kings, gift us tales like the **Ocean Churning**, **Vamana Avatar**, **Gajendra Moksha**, and **Mohini's Amrita deception**, where Vishnu's avatars balance the cosmos. The **Mahabharata**, an epic of family, war, and dharma, offers stories like **Draupadi's swayamvara**, **Yayati and Devayani**, **Arjuna's quest**, and **King Shibi's compassion**, each exploring human virtues and struggles. The **Ramayana**, a saga of love and duty, brings us **Rama and Sita's journey**, a timeless ode to devotion. The **Upanishads**, philosophical treasures, give us **Nachiketa and Yama**, a dialogue on the soul's immortality. Other texts, like the Devi Mahatmya, inspire **Durga's triumph**, while oral traditions enrich tales like **Ganesha's birth** and **Krishna's leelas**.

These stories span cosmic battles and intimate moments. We witness the **Kurma Avatar** supporting a churning ocean, **Varaha Avatar** lifting the earth from demonic depths, and **Matsya Avatar** saving humanity from a flood. We walk with **Bhagiratha** to bring Ganga to earth, stand with **Parashurama** as he purges tyranny, and weep with **Harishchandra** as he clings to truth. We marvel at **Shiva and Parvati's love**, **Savitri's defiance of death**, and **Shakuntala's reunion with Dushyanta**. Each tale, rooted in its source, is retold with vivid imagery and emotional depth, inviting you to see Durga's spear flash, hear Krishna's flute, or feel Nachiketa's fearless gaze.

The Heart of the Stories

What makes these stories endure? Their heart lies in their universal themes, which speak to every soul, regardless of time or place. **Devotion** pulses through tales like **Prahlada's faith**, **Gajendra's surrender**, and **Markandeya's embrace of Shiva**, showing that a pure heart draws the divine near. **Dharma**, the law of righteousness, guides **Rama's exile**, **Arjuna's quest**, and **Harishchandra's truth**, teaching that duty, though painful, upholds life's order. **Courage** shines in **Durga's battle**, **Parashurama's wrath**, and **Nachiketa's questions**, proving that bravery is both physical and spiritual. **Sacrifice**, from **Shibi's flesh** to **Savitri's love**, reveals that giving without expectation is the highest act of love. **Wisdom**, found in **Yayati's awakening** and **Yama's teachings**, illuminates the path beyond fleeting pleasures to eternal truth.

These themes are not abstract; they are lived in the characters' joys and sorrows. I see Rama's heart breaking in Sita's abduction, Savitri's feet bleeding as she follows Yama, and Yayati's weary sigh as he sheds youth's illusion. I feel Draupadi's fire, Shibi's blood pooling, and Nachiketa's curiosity piercing death's veil. These stories are mirrors, reflecting our own struggles—love tested, truth challenged, faith wavered. They assure us we are not alone, that gods and heroes have walked these paths, leaving footprints of grace.

The Journey of Compilation

Compiling these stories has been a pilgrimage, each tale a step closer to the divine. As I wove these narratives, I felt like a bard by that banyan tree, my voice trembling with Krishna's mischief, my heart heavy with Harishchandra's loss. I've danced with Ganesha's joy, trembled with Ahalya's redemption, and stood in awe with Arjuna before Shiva. These stories have been my teachers, revealing my own desires, fears, and hopes. Yayati's chase mirrored my restless moments; Gajendra's prayer taught me trust; Shibi's mercy urged me to give freely.

Translating these tales into English was a delicate task, like carrying a flame across a river. I sought to preserve their cultural nuances—the scent of lotuses in Gajendra's lake, the rhythm of Shiva's tandava, the weight of Draupadi's saree. Yet, I aimed for simplicity, ensuring readers new to these texts could feel Mohini's enchantment or Nachiketa's truth without stumbling over unfamiliar terms. Each story is a tapestry of vivid imagery, emotional depth, and spiritual insight, inviting you to live its moments.

An Invitation to Readers

This book is not just to read but to experience. As you turn its pages, let yourself weep with Harishchandra, laugh with Krishna, and wonder with Nachiketa. See the stories' colors—Durga's red saree, Vishnu's blue skin, Ganga's silver flow. Hear their sounds—Rama's bowstring, Shiva's damaru, Arjuna's conch. Feel their heartbeats—Savitri's love, Shibi's mercy, Yayati's regret. These tales are alive, ready to walk with you through life's joys and trials.

For new readers, start with an open heart; no prior knowledge is needed. Let Ganesha, remover of obstacles, guide your journey. For devotees, rediscover these tales as prayers, each story a mantra of dharma. For storytellers, share these narratives with children, friends, or communities, keeping their flame alive. Whether you read by a quiet lamp or under a starry sky, let these stories be your companions, whispering truths that endure.

A Note of Gratitude

I offer my gratitude to the sages who first sang these tales, to the texts that preserved them, and to the countless voices—grandparents, priests, performers—who kept them alive. I thank you, dear reader, for joining me under this banyan tree, for listening as I poured my soul into these pages. Your presence makes these stories breathe; their wisdom shared like a sacred offering.

As you begin this journey, I pray these tales light your path. May Vishnu's conch call you to courage, Shiva's trident guard your truth, and Durga's spear slay your doubts. May Krishna's flute bring joy, Rama's love brings peace, and Nachiketa's wisdom bring clarity. Welcome to this tapestry of stories, where gods and mortals weave a song of eternity.

INDEX

About the Author

I'm Rajnish Kumar—a storyteller at heart and a lifelong admirer of India's rich spiritual and cultural heritage. This book, *Faith and Fables: Timeless Hindu Tales*, is a humble effort to bring forward thirty stories from the vast world of Hindu mythology—drawn from sacred texts like the Purāṇas, Vedas, Upanishads, and epics—retold in a way that is simple, meaningful, and relevant to today's readers, especially the younger generation.

Over the years, I have found myself deeply moved by the timeless lessons hidden in these ancient tales—stories of gods and sages, demons and devotees. I've come to believe that these aren't just old stories—they are living truths, passed down for generations to guide, inspire, and awaken something within us.

I've tried to stay true to the original spirit of the stories while retelling them in a language and tone that feels approachable to readers of all ages.

In many ways, this book is part of my personal journey—a way of staying connected to the roots that have shaped me and offering something heartfelt in return.

I hope these tales bring you the same joy, wonder, and reflection they have brought me.

— RAJNISH KUMAR

Famous Stories from the Hindu Puranas

The Puranas are like a treasure chest of ancient stories, filled with tales of gods, goddesses, heroes, and cosmic adventures. They're not just stories—they're windows into the heart of Hindu beliefs, teaching us about life, love, and the divine. Growing up, I'd sit wide-eyed as my grandmother spun these tales, her voice weaving magic into the air. Now, I want to share that magic with you. These stories come from the Puranas, sacred texts like the Vishnu Purana, Shiva Purana, and Devi Bhagavata Purana, trusted by millions for centuries. I've picked selected famous ones for this book. They're written in simple words, as if I'm sitting across from you, telling them from my heart. Let's dive in.

Story 1: The Churning of the Ocean (Samudra Manthan)

Long ago, when the world was young and the gods and demons still walked among us, there was a time when everything felt out of balance. I can almost picture it: the skies were dim, the rivers sluggish, and even the gods in their golden palaces of Swarga felt weak. It all started with a curse, as so many great stories do. Sage Durvasa, known for his fiery temper, had gifted a garland to Indra, the king of the gods. But Indra, proud and careless, tossed it onto his elephant, who trampled it. Furious, Durvasa cursed the gods to lose their strength and immortality. And just like that, the devas became as frail as mortals. The demons, or asuras, saw their chance to seize control. Desperate, the gods turned to Lord Vishnu, the preserver of the universe, for help. What followed was an adventure so grand, it changed the world forever—the Churning of the Ocean.

The gods gathered in Vishnu's radiant presence, their faces pale with worry. Vishnu, calm as always, smiled and said, "Fear not. The nectar of immortality, amrita, lies hidden in the depths of the Kshirasagara, the Ocean of Milk. You must churn this ocean to bring it forth. But you cannot do it alone. You'll need the asuras' strength." The gods exchanged uneasy glances. Work with their enemies? It seemed impossible. But Vishnu's wisdom was never wrong, so they agreed.

The plan was set. The gods and demons would use Mount Mandara as a churning rod and Vasuki, the great serpent king, as the rope. They'd spin the mountain in the ocean, like churning butter from cream, until the treasures hidden within emerged. I can imagine the scene: the vast, shimmering Ocean of Milk stretching endlessly, its waves glowing under the starry sky. Mount Mandara, tall and majestic, was uprooted by the gods and demons working together—a rare sight, their hands calloused but united for a common goal.

But there was a problem. As they placed Mandara in the ocean, it began to sink, too heavy for the waters to hold. The gods and demons panicked, their shouts echoing across the waves. Just then, Vishnu took the form of Kurma, a giant tortoise. Slipping beneath the mountain, he balanced it on his sturdy back. I like to think of Kurma's kind eyes peeking out, steady and patient, as the mountain rested safely. With Mandara secure, the churning could begin.

Vasuki coiled himself around the mountain, his scales glinting like emeralds. The gods grabbed his tail, and the demons, ever competitive, insisted on holding his head. "The head is nobler!" they argued. Vishnu, watching from afar, only smiled. The churning started, slow at first, then faster. The gods pulled, the demons tugged, and Mandara spun, stirring the ocean into frothy waves. Days turned into weeks, then years. The effort was immense—sweat dripped from their brows, and Vasuki's writhing body ached.

But then, disaster struck. Vasuki, exhausted, began to spew venom from his mouth. The poison, called Halahala, was so deadly it scorched the air, turning the sky black. The gods and demons froze, coughing and choking as the poison spread. Even the ocean seemed to tremble. In that moment of despair, Lord Shiva appeared, his matted hair swaying, his presence like a cool breeze. Without a word, he scooped up the poison in his hands and drank it. I can almost see Parvati, his wife, gasping beside him, her heart pounding. To save Shiva from the poison's wrath, she clutched his throat, stopping it from spreading. Shiva's throat turned blue, earning him the name Neelkanth, the Blue-Throated One. Calmly, he returned to his meditation, as if saving the universe was just another day's work.

With the poison gone, the churning resumed. The ocean began to yield its treasures, each more wondrous than the last. First came Kamadhenu, the wish-fulfilling cow, her gentle eyes promising abundance. The gods and demons stared in awe as she floated ashore. Next emerged Uchhaishravas, a magnificent seven-headed horse, white as moonlight. Then came the Airavata, a splendid elephant with four tusks, claimed by Indra. A celestial tree, Parijata, bloomed with flowers that never wilted, filling the air with sweetness. And there was Lakshmi, the goddess of wealth, radiant in golden robes. She glanced at Vishnu, her eternal consort, and placed a garland around his neck, choosing him as her husband. The gods cheered, but the demons grumbled, their eyes fixed on the next treasure.

Then came Dhanvantari, the divine physician, holding a golden pot. Inside was the amrita, the nectar of immortality. The demons' eyes gleamed with greed. "It's ours!" they roared, snatching the pot and running. The gods chased them, but the demons were too fast. Chaos erupted—shouts, curses, and the clash of weapons. Vishnu, ever the strategist, transformed into Mohini, a woman of breathtaking beauty. Her smile was enough to stop the demons in their tracks. "Why fight?" she cooed. "Let me distribute the nectar fairly."

The demons, enchanted, handed her the pot. Mohini lined up the gods and demons in two rows. With a twinkle in her eye, she began serving the gods first, pouring the sweet nectar into their cups. The demons waited, mesmerized by her charm. But one demon, Rahu, grew suspicious. Disguising himself as a god, he slipped into their row and sipped the nectar. The sun and moon gods noticed and alerted Mohini. In a flash, Vishnu resumed his form and hurled his Sudarshana Chakra, slicing Rahu's head from his body. But the nectar had already made Rahu immortal. His head lived on, forever chasing the sun and moon, causing eclipses.

By the time the demons realized Mohini's trick, the gods had drunk most of the nectar. Furious, they attacked, but the gods, now immortal, fought back with renewed strength. The battle raged across the heavens, but the gods prevailed, driving the demons back to their underworld. Peace returned to the universe, and the Ocean of Milk sparkled once more, its treasures shared among the worlds.

And so, the Churning of the Ocean came to an end, a tale of teamwork, trickery, and divine grace. I love this story because it reminds me that even in the darkest times, there's hope if we work together and trust in something bigger. The gods and demons, so different, found a way to share a goal, even if just for a moment. And Vishnu, Shiva, and the others—they're not just gods; they're like family, stepping in when we need them most. This story, from the Vishnu Purana, is told in temples and homes across India, a reminder that life, like the ocean, holds treasures if we dare to churn it.

Story 2: The Birth of Ganesha

There's something special about Lord Ganesha, isn't there? With his elephant head, round belly, and mischievous eyes, he feels like a friend who's always there, ready to clear our troubles. Every festival, every new beginning, we call his name first. But have you ever wondered how Ganesha came to be? Let me take you back to a time when the gods lived in the snowy peaks of Kailasa, and a mother's love created one of the most beloved deities. This is the story of Ganesha's birth, a tale from the Shiva Purana that's as heartwarming as it is divine.

High on Mount Kailasa, where the air sparkles with purity, lived Lord Shiva and Goddess Parvati. Their home was a paradise of icy peaks and blooming lotuses, a place where time seemed to stand still. Shiva, the great yogi, was often lost in meditation, his mind soaring beyond the stars. Parvati, radiant and kind, managed their divine household, her laughter echoing through the caves. But even goddesses have moments of loneliness, and Parvati sometimes wished for someone to keep her company while Shiva was away.

One day, as Parvati prepared for her bath, she realized she had no one to guard the door. Shiva's attendants, the ganas, were loyal but always followed his orders, not hers. "I need someone who's mine," she thought, her heart stirring with a mother's instinct. Sitting by a stream, she gathered turmeric paste from her body—soft, golden, and fragrant. With love and care, she molded it into the shape of a boy, small but sturdy, with bright eyes and a gentle smile. As she gazed at him, she poured her divine energy into the figure, and in a flash of light, the boy came to life.

He blinked up at her, his face full of innocence. "Mother," he said, his voice sweet as honey. Parvati's heart melted. She named him Ganesha, meaning "lord of the ganas," and hugged him tightly. "My son," she said, "you'll guard our home and be my joy." Ganesha nodded, eager to please. Parvati gave him a staff and said, "Stand by the door while I bathe, and let no one enter without my permission." Ganesha puffed out his chest, proud of his duty, and took his place outside the cave.

Inside, Parvati stepped into the warm, lotus-scented water, feeling at peace knowing her son stood guard. But she hadn't counted on Shiva's return. After months of meditation, Shiva strode toward Kailasa, his trident gleaming, his ganas chattering behind him. He was eager to see Parvati, his heart light with love. As he approached the cave, he saw a strange boy blocking the entrance, staff in hand. "Who are you?" Shiva asked, surprised. No one had ever stopped him before.

"I'm Ganesha, son of Parvati," the boy replied boldly. "Mother's bathing, and no one may enter." Shiva frowned. Son? He had no son. The ganas snickered, thinking it a prank. "Step aside, child," Shiva said, his voice gentle but firm. But Ganesha stood his ground, his small frame unwavering. "I obey only my mother," he said. The ganas gasped at his audacity, but Ganesha's eyes shone with loyalty.

Shiva's patience wore thin. He was the destroyer, after all, and not used to being defied. "Move, or face my wrath," he warned. Ganesha gripped his staff tighter, unafraid. A scuffle broke out. The ganas charged, but Ganesha, fueled by his mother's power, swung his staff with surprising strength, sending them tumbling. Shiva's temper flared. Drawing his trident, he faced the boy in combat. Ganesha fought bravely, his heart full of duty, but he was no match for Shiva's cosmic might. In a moment of fury, Shiva struck, and Ganesha's head flew from his body, landing far away.

A terrible silence followed. Parvati, sensing something wrong, rushed out of the cave. When she saw her son's lifeless body, her scream shook the mountains. "Shiva, what have you done?" she cried, tears streaming down her face. Shiva, seeing her anguish, realized his mistake. His heart sank. He hadn't known the boy was Parvati's creation, her son. "I'll make this right," he promised, his voice heavy with regret.

Shiva turned to his ganas. "Find the head of the first creature you see, facing north," he ordered. The ganas hurried off, their hearts racing. They soon spotted an elephant, wise and noble, its trunk raised northward. With respect, they took its head and brought it to Shiva. Gently, Shiva placed the elephant's head on Ganesha's body, chanting sacred mantras. He poured divine nectar over the boy, and life returned. Ganesha's eyes fluttered open, his new head gleaming, his trunk curling playfully.

Parvati ran to him, sobbing with joy. "My son!" she exclaimed, embracing him. Ganesha smiled, his elephant face radiant. Shiva, moved by the scene, declared, "From now on, Ganesha will be our son, loved by all. He'll be the remover of obstacles, worshipped first in every prayer." The gods, who had gathered to watch, showered flowers from the heavens. Brahma, Vishnu, and the others blessed Ganesha, granting him wisdom, strength, and devotion.

But the story doesn't end there. Ganesha, now wise beyond his years, became the guardian of beginnings. One day, the gods debated who was the greatest among them. To settle it, they agreed on a race around the universe. While the others sped off on their divine mounts, Ganesha, with his round belly and modest mouse vahana, circled his parents, Shiva and Parvati. "You are my universe," he said simply. Touched by his wisdom, the gods declared him the winner, naming him the lord of knowledge.

Ganesha's life was full of adventures, but his birth was the spark that made him who he is. He loves sweets, especially modakas, and his mouse friend scurries by his side, nibbling crumbs. Temples across India hum with his name, and every new venture—be it a wedding or a journey—starts with his blessing. I like to think Ganesha's laughter echoes in our hearts, reminding us to face challenges with courage and love.

And that's how Ganesha came to be, a story of a mother's love, a father's redemption, and a boy who became a god. From the Shiva Purana, this tale is told in every home, every temple, especially during Ganesh Chaturthi. It's a reminder that even mistakes can lead to miracles, and that family—divine or human—holds the power to heal. Ganesha's elephant head isn't just a mark of his birth; it's a symbol of wisdom and kindness, guiding us through life's obstacles.

Story 3: The Birth of Krishna

Whenever I hear Krishna's name, a smile creeps across my face, and I can almost hear the soft melody of his flute dancing in the air. Krishna isn't just a god; he's a friend, a guide, a spark of joy. His stories fill the lanes of Mathura and Vrindavan with life even today. But the sweetest of them all is the story of his birth, found in the Bhagavata Purana. It's a tale of a stormy night, a mother and father's love, and a wicked king's fear. This story always reminds me that even in the darkest moments, a tiny ray of hope can change everything. So, let's travel back to that night when a baby was born to save the world.

Long ago, the land of Mathura was under a shadow of fear. King Kansa, a cruel and mighty ruler, held sway over the city. His power was so great that people trembled at his name. But deep inside, Kansa was always afraid. It all began on the day his sister Devaki married Vasudeva, a kind and noble man. As they rode through Mathura in their wedding procession, a voice boomed from the heavens. "Kansa!" it declared. "The eighth child of Devaki and Vasudeva will be your doom!" Kansa's face turned pale. In a fit of rage, he drew his sword to kill his own sister. But Vasudeva stepped forward, his voice steady. "Spare her, Kansa," he pleaded. "I promise to hand over every child we have to you. Just let Devaki live."

Kansa agreed, but his heart was cold. He threw Devaki and Vasudeva into a dark dungeon in Mathura, surrounded by iron bars and guarded by fierce soldiers. I can imagine how grim that cell must have been—cold stone walls, the air heavy with despair. Yet, Devaki and Vasudeva held onto each other, their love a flicker of light in the darkness. One by one, six of their children were born, and each time, Kansa's cruelty took them away. Devaki's tears fell silently, but Kansa's fear only grew. "Was that the eighth child?" he wondered after each loss, his heart restless. But the seventh child was special. It was Balarama, an incarnation of Lord Vishnu's serpent, Sheshnaga. Lord Vishnu, the preserver of the universe, was weaving a plan to save the world from Kansa's tyranny. He called upon Yogamaya, his divine power, to help. In a miracle, Yogamaya transferred Balarama from Devaki's womb to Rohini's in Gokul, far from Kansa's reach. When Kansa learned that Devaki's seventh child had "disappeared," his fear turned to fury. "This is some magic!" he roared, tightening the guards around the dungeon.

Then came the night of the eighth child. The sky was alive with dark clouds, lightning flashing, and rain pouring down like a waterfall. Inside the dungeon, Devaki and Vasudeva prayed with all their hearts. Suddenly, a radiant light filled the cell, chasing away the shadows. Before them stood Lord Vishnu, his four arms holding a conch, discus, mace, and lotus. His presence was like a warm breeze. "Do not fear," he said, his voice calm yet powerful.

"I will be born as your eighth child, named Krishna, and I will end Kansa's reign."

Devaki and Vasudeva's eyes sparkled with hope. That very night, Devaki gave birth to a beautiful baby boy. His skin was as dark as a monsoon cloud, his eyes twinkled like stars, and his tiny smile lit up the dungeon. A sweet fragrance filled the air. But Devaki's heart sank with fear. "Kansa will take him too," she whispered, tears streaming down her face. Just then, Yogamaya appeared. "Vasudeva," she said, "take this child to Gokul, where Yashoda and Nanda will raise him. Bring their newborn daughter back here."

Vasudeva gently placed baby Krishna in a wicker basket, his heart torn between love and fear. I can picture that moment—a father cradling his newborn, stepping into a stormy night, driven by hope. As Vasudeva left the dungeon, a miracle unfolded. The iron bars swung open on their own, and the guards fell into a deep sleep. Outside, the Yamuna River roared, its waves wild and fierce. Vasudeva held the basket above his head and stepped into the raging waters, rain lashing his face. He didn't falter, his love for Krishna stronger than any storm.

Then, another wonder happened. Sheshnaga, the great serpent, appeared, spreading his hoods like an umbrella to shield Vasudeva and Krishna from the rain. The Yamuna calmed her waves, parting to make a path for them. I imagine that scene—a father, a tiny baby, and a mighty serpent, walking together through the storm. It's a picture of courage and divine care. In

Gokul, Vasudeva reached the home of Yashoda and Nanda. Yashoda had just given birth to a baby girl. Quietly, Vasudeva placed Krishna beside Yashoda and took the girl in his basket.

Back in Mathura, he returned to the dungeon with the girl. At dawn, the guards awoke and alerted Kansa that the eighth child was born. Kansa stormed in, his eyes wild with fear. "This is the one!" he shouted, snatching the baby girl. He raised her to strike, but something miraculous happened. The girl slipped from his grasp and rose into the sky. She transformed into Yogamaya, a radiant goddess. "Kansa!" she thundered. "The child who will destroy you is alive and beyond your reach!" With that, she vanished.

Kansa trembled, his heart gripped by dread. He sent his soldiers to kill every newborn in Mathura and Gokul, but Krishna was safe in Yashoda's arms. In Gokul, the baby giggled, his tiny hands waving, filling the village with joy. "Our Lala," Yashoda called him, her heart overflowing with love. Nanda smiled, unaware that the child in their home was divine. Gokul came alive with the sound of cowbells and laughter, and Krishna's story began—a tale of butter-stealing, dancing with gopis, and one day, facing Kansa. But that's for another time.

Krishna's birth wasn't just the arrival of a child. It was a promise—that no matter how powerful evil seems, goodness will always triumph. In Gokul, where the air was filled with the scent of cows and the tune of flutes, Krishna began his playful journey. I think of Yashoda, rocking her little one, not knowing he would grow to guide the world. Krishna's smile held a magic that still lives in our hearts today.

And so, Krishna was born, a story woven with love, sacrifice, and miracles. From the Bhagavata Purana, this tale is told in every home and temple, especially during Janmashtami. It reminds me that even in the darkest nights, when all seems lost, a small light can change everything. Krishna's birth was more than a child's arrival; it was the birth of hope, teaching us that love and courage can defeat any fear. Whenever I see the lamps glowing on Janmashtami night, I feel Krishna's flute calling, whispering joy and strength to us all.

Story 4: The Slaying of Mahishasura by Maa Durga

The name of Mother Durga fills my heart with a sense of strength, like a warm hand holding mine in tough times. With her ten arms, lion mount, and radiant face, she feels like a mother who hears every call from her children. In the Devi Bhagavata Purana, there's a story about her that I hold close—the slaying of Mahishasura. It's a tale of good conquering evil, of a goddess who stood tall against a demon's tyranny. When I hear this story, I feel Durga's power beside me, urging me to be brave. Let's step back to a time when a demon shook the heavens and earth, and a divine mother rose to answer the call.

Once upon a time, a demon named Mahishasura spread terror across the three worlds—heaven, earth, and the netherworld. He wasn't an ordinary demon. Half-buffalo, half-human, his strength could make mountains tremble. Mahishasura had won a boon from Lord Brahma: no man, god, or demon could kill him. With this, he thought himself invincible. His arrogance grew, and he led his massive army to attack heaven. I can picture the chaos—dark clouds covering the sky, the ground shaking under his army's march.

The gods, led by Indra, Agni, and Varuna, fought bravely to protect their home. But Mahishasura's power was too great. He defeated them, driving the gods out of heaven.

The gods, driven from their heavenly abode, were filled with despair. I can imagine their faces—once radiant with divine light, now shadowed with fear and defeat. They gathered before the trinity of gods—Brahma, Vishnu, and Shiva—pleading for help. "Mahishasura has taken everything," they cried. "Save us!" The three great gods exchanged a knowing glance, their resolve firm. They decided to combine their powers to create a force strong enough to defeat the demon. Brahma offered his creative energy, Vishnu his protective strength, and Shiva his destructive might. The other gods joined in, offering their own powers—Indra's thunderbolt, Agni's fire, Vayu's speed.

A dazzling light erupted, so bright it lit up the entire universe. From that light emerged a goddess—Durga. She was breathtaking. Her ten arms held an array of weapons—a trident, discus, sword, bow, and mace. Her face glowed like the sun, her eyes filled with compassion and power. Beneath her stood a majestic lion, its roar shaking the mountains. I can almost see that moment—a goddess born from the collective strength of the gods, ready to face evil itself. The gods bowed before her, their hearts lifted by her presence.

"Mother," they said, "save us." Durga smiled, her voice as gentle as a breeze yet firm as a rock. "Mahishasura's end is certain. I have heard your call." With that, she mounted her lion and rode toward the battlefield. Word reached Mahishasura that a goddess was coming to challenge him. He laughed, his voice booming. “A woman defeat me?” he scoffed. “My boon makes me immortal!” But he didn’t know his boon only protected him from men, gods, and demons—not from a goddess.

The battlefield was set, a vast plain where Mahishasura stood with his fearsome army—demons with teeth like swords and weapons that spat fire. Durga descended onto the field, her lion’s mane flowing, her presence sending a shiver through the demons’ ranks. The battle began, and it was like a storm unleashed. Durga’s ten arms moved with such grace and speed, it was as if she were dancing. Her trident pierced through demons, her discus sliced through their ranks, and her lion’s roar scattered the enemy like leaves in the wind. I can picture the scene—her golden armor gleaming, her weapons a blur, and her lion charging with unmatched ferocity.

Mahishasura was cunning. He changed forms to confuse her—now a buffalo, now a lion, now an elephant. But Durga was unshaken. When he became a buffalo, her sword met his charge. When he turned into a lion, her own lion pounced, pinning him down. The battle raged for nine days and nine nights. I imagine the intensity of it—Durga’s unwavering strength against Mahishasura’s relentless trickery, the earth trembling under their clash, the skies watching in awe.

On the tenth day, Mahishasura took his true form—a colossal buffalo, its horns reaching for the sky. He charged at Durga, the ground shaking with each step. But Durga stood tall, her eyes blazing with determination. She signaled her lion, which leaped at Mahishasura, claws bared. With a swift motion, Durga raised her trident and struck, the weapon piercing the demon's chest. Mahishasura let out a terrible cry and collapsed, his reign of terror ended at last.

Joy swept through heaven and earth. The gods sang Durga's praises, showering her with flowers from the skies. "Jai Mata Di!" their voices echoed. Durga smiled, her presence as warm as a mother's embrace. "Whenever my children call, I will come," she promised. Then, mounting her lion, she returned to her divine abode. From that day, the festival of Navratri was born, where for nine nights, people worship Mother Durga, and on the tenth day, they celebrate her victory as Vijayadashami.

This story of Durga isn't just about a battle. It's a reminder of the strength within us all, a spark that can overcome any darkness. Whenever I see an idol of Durga, her lion proud and her weapons gleaming, I feel her whispering, "Be fearless, for I am with you."

And so, Mother Durga slew Mahishasura, a tale of power, courage, and triumph. From the Devi Bhagavata Purana, this story rings out during Navratri in temples and homes across India. It reminds me that no matter how big the challenge, if we tap into our inner strength, nothing can stop us. Durga's roar still echoes in our hearts, urging us to face our fears and emerge victorious. Every Navratri, when I see her idol adorned with flowers, I feel her strength, as if she's saying, "You are never alone."

Story 5: Narasimha and Prahlada

The name Prahlada brings a quiet strength to my heart, like a candle glowing steady in a storm. His story, found in the Bhagavata Purana, is one of pure devotion—a young boy who loved Lord Vishnu so deeply that no fear could touch him. It's also the story of Narasimha, Vishnu's fierce yet loving avatar, who came to protect his devotee. This tale always reminds me that faith can move mountains, even when the world seems against you. Let's travel back to a time when a demon king ruled with an iron fist, and a child's love for God changed everything.

Long ago, the demon king Hiranyakashipu ruled the three worlds—heaven, earth, and the netherworld. He was no ordinary king. His power was immense, earned through years of intense penance to Lord Brahma. In his pride, he demanded a boon: that he could not be killed by man or beast, inside or outside, during day or night, on land or in the sky, with any weapon. Brahma granted the boon, and Hiranyakashipu believed himself immortal. I can picture him, towering and fierce, his golden crown glinting as he declared, "I am greater than the gods!" He forbade worship of anyone but himself, and his name echoed in fear across the land.

But in his own palace lived someone who defied him—his son, Prahlada. From the moment he was born, Prahlada was different.

His heart was filled with love for Lord Vishnu, the preserver of the universe. As a tiny child, he would sing Vishnu's names, his voice soft but clear, like a stream flowing through a forest. I imagine him sitting under a tree, his eyes closed, lost in thoughts of his beloved God. Hiranyakashipu, however, hated Vishnu. Years before, Vishnu, as the boar Varaha, had killed Hiranyakashipu's brother, Hiranyaksha. The demon king's heart burned with revenge, and Prahlada's devotion felt like a betrayal.

Hiranyakashipu tried to change his son. He sent Prahlada to the best teachers, demons who taught him to worship the king. But Prahlada's heart was unswayed. "Vishnu is everywhere," he told his teachers. "He's in the trees, the rivers, and even in you." The teachers were furious and reported to Hiranyakashipu. "Your son speaks only of Vishnu!" they said. The king roared, summoning Prahlada to his grand throne room, its pillars gleaming with gold. "Who is this Vishnu you worship?" he demanded.

Prahlada, small but fearless, looked into his father's eyes. "Vishnu is the creator of all, the one who loves and protects us," he said calmly. Hiranyakashipu's face twisted with rage. "I am the only god here!" he shouted. "Stop this nonsense, or you'll pay with your life!" But Prahlada only smiled, his heart steady. "Vishnu is my strength," he replied. I can feel the courage in that moment—a young boy standing before a fearsome king, his faith brighter than any threat.

Hiranyakashipu decided to teach Prahlada a lesson. He ordered his guards to kill the boy. First, they threw Prahlada into a pit of venomous snakes. But the snakes curled around him gently, as if greeting a friend. Then, they pushed him off a cliff, but the wind caught him and set him softly on the ground. They tried to burn him in a blazing fire, but Prahlada sat unharmed, chanting Vishnu's name, the flames cool as a breeze around him. Each time, Hiranyakashipu grew angrier, but Prahlada's faith only deepened. I imagine him, his face serene, whispering, "Narayana, you are with me."

Hiranyakashipu's sister, Holika, had a boon that fire could not burn her. She devised a plan. "I'll sit in a fire with Prahlada on my lap," she said. "The flames will spare me but destroy him." A massive pyre was built, its flames licking the sky. Holika sat with Prahlada, smirking. But as the fire roared, Prahlada chanted Vishnu's name, his voice rising above the crackle. Miraculously, the flames turned against Holika, reducing her to ashes, while Prahlada walked out untouched, his heart full of gratitude. The people watching gasped, whispering, "This boy is blessed!" Today, we celebrate this miracle during Holi, lighting bonfires to honor Prahlada's faith.

Hiranyakashipu's fury knew no bounds. One evening, as the sun dipped below the horizon, he dragged Prahlada to his throne room. "Where is your Vishnu?" he bellowed, his voice shaking the walls. "If he's everywhere, show him to me!" Prahlada looked around, his eyes calm. "He's in this pillar, in you, in me," he said, pointing to a massive stone pillar nearby. Hiranyakashipu laughed, a cruel sound. “In this pillar? Let’s see!” He struck the pillar with his sword, expecting nothing.

But the pillar split open with a thunderous roar. From it emerged Narasimha, Vishnu’s fierce avatar—neither man nor beast, but a lion-headed being with a human body. His eyes blazed like fire, his claws gleamed, and his roar shook the heavens. I can picture the scene—Hiranyakashipu frozen, his boon useless against this divine form. Narasimha lifted the demon king and carried him to the threshold of the palace, neither inside nor outside. At twilight, neither day nor night, he placed Hiranyakashipu on his lap, neither on land nor in the sky. With his claws, no ordinary weapon, Narasimha tore the demon apart, ending his reign of terror.

The gods and people cheered, but Prahlada only bowed before Narasimha, tears of love in his eyes. “My Lord, you came for me,” he whispered. Narasimha’s fierce face softened, and he placed a gentle hand on Prahlada’s head. “Your faith called me,” he said. “You will rule with love and righteousness.” With that, Narasimha vanished, leaving peace in his wake. Prahlada became a wise and kind king, his heart forever tied to Vishnu. His story spread, inspiring countless devotees to trust in God’s protection.

This tale of Prahlada and Narasimha is more than a story of good over evil. It’s a song of devotion, a reminder that love for the divine can make us fearless. I think of Prahlada’s small voice, singing Vishnu’s name, and it fills me with warmth, like a hug from someone who believes in you.

And so, Narasimha came to save Prahlada, a story of faith, courage, and divine love. From the Bhagavata Purana, this tale is sung in temples and homes, especially during Narasimha Jayanti. It reminds me that when we hold onto love and trust, no darkness can touch us. Prahlada's devotion was a light that called God himself, teaching us that faith can conquer any fear. Whenever I see an image of Narasimha, his fierce yet loving eyes, I feel Prahlada's courage in my heart, whispering that we're never alone.

Story 6: The Marriage of Shiva and Parvati

The love story of Shiva and Parvati feels like a warm melody, one that lingers in the heart long after it's heard. Found in the Shiva Purana, it's a tale of devotion, patience, and a love so deep it spans lifetimes. Shiva, the meditative yogi, and Parvati, the radiant goddess, seem so different, yet their union is the heartbeat of the universe. This story always makes me smile, reminding me that true love finds a way, no matter the obstacles. Let's journey to the snowy peaks of the Himalayas, where a goddess's love awakened the heart of the great ascetic.

High in the Himalayas, where the air sparkles with purity, lived Lord Shiva, the destroyer and creator of worlds. His home was Mount Kailasa, a paradise of ice and lotuses, where he spent his days in deep meditation. Shiva was unlike any other god—his body smeared with ash, his hair matted, a serpent around his neck, and his eyes closed in cosmic bliss. I can picture him, sitting still as a rock, his presence calming the winds. But once, Shiva had a wife—Sati, the daughter of King Daksha. Their love was pure, but it ended in tragedy. Daksha, who disliked Shiva's wild ways, insulted him at a grand sacrifice. Sati, unable to bear her father's scorn, gave up her life in the sacrificial fire, leaving Shiva heartbroken.

Shiva retreated to Kailasa, lost in meditation, his heart closed to the world. But Sati's soul was reborn as Parvati, the daughter of Himavan, the king of the Himalayas, and his wife, Mena. From childhood, Parvati was drawn to Shiva. She heard tales of the great yogi, his trident gleaming, his dance creating and destroying universes. "He's my lord," she whispered to herself, her young heart already his. I imagine her as a little girl, weaving flower garlands, dreaming of the day she'd meet Shiva.

As Parvati grew, her beauty was unmatched, her face glowing like the moon, her kindness warming everyone around her. But her heart belonged to Shiva alone. She told her parents, "I will marry only Shiva." Himavan was worried. "Shiva is an ascetic," he said. "He cares for nothing but meditation." But Parvati was firm. "I will win his heart," she said, her eyes shining with determination. She set out for Kailasa, leaving her palace for the rugged mountains, her resolve as strong as the peaks.

Parvati began serving Shiva, bringing him flowers, fruits, and water from sacred streams. She swept the ground near his meditation spot, her hands gentle but steady. Shiva, deep in trance, didn't notice her. Days turned to months, then years, but Parvati never wavered. I can see her, dressed in simple clothes, her face serene, tending to Shiva's needs with love. Her friends urged her to return home, but she smiled. "My heart is here," she said. Her devotion was so pure that even the animals of Kailasa—

deer, birds, and snakes—grew fond of her, staying close as she worked.

The gods, watching from heaven, grew anxious. The demon Tarakasura was wreaking havoc, and only a son born to Shiva and Parvati could defeat him. But Shiva's meditation was unbreakable. The gods sent Kamadeva, the god of love, to stir Shiva's heart. Kamadeva, with his bow of sugarcane and arrows of flowers, stood before Shiva and shot an arrow of desire. For a moment, Shiva's eyes flickered. But then, his third eye opened, blazing with fire, and Kamadeva was reduced to ashes. I imagine Parvati's heart sinking, yet her resolve growing stronger. Kamadeva's wife, Rati, wept, and Shiva, moved by her grief, promised Kamadeva would live on

without form, spreading love.

Parvati realized love alone wasn't enough. She decided to win Shiva through penance, just as he had won his powers. She went to a forest grove, stood on one leg, and meditated on Shiva, her body enduring heat, cold, and rain. Her lips whispered his name, her heart one with his. Her tapas, or penance, grew so intense that the earth trembled, and a divine light surrounded her. The gods, awestruck, pleaded with Shiva. "See her devotion," they said. Finally, Shiva opened his eyes and descended to the grove.

Disguised as a sage, Shiva tested Parvati. "Why waste your beauty on that wild yogi?" he asked. "Shiva cares for no one." Parvati's eyes blazed. "He is my lord, the soul of the universe. I will have no other." Shiva smiled, revealing his true form—blue-throated, radiant, his trident in hand. "You have won me, Parvati," he said, his voice soft. Parvati's heart soared, tears of joy in her eyes. I can feel that moment—their eyes meeting, a love that had waited lifetimes now fulfilled.

The marriage was a cosmic celebration. The gods arrived, led by Brahma and Vishnu. Himavan adorned Kailasa with flowers and jewels. Parvati, dressed in red, glowed like a sunrise, her hands trembling as she held a garland. Shiva, adorned with serpents and ash, looked at her with love, his heart no longer closed. Brahma performed the rituals, and the heavens showered petals. I imagine the joy—gandharvas singing, apsaras dancing, and the mountains echoing with cheers. Shiva and Parvati circled the sacred fire, their union sealing a bond that would bring balance to the universe.

Their son, Kartikeya, was born later, defeating Tarakasura as foretold. But the marriage itself was a miracle, a testament to love's power. Shiva and Parvati returned to Kailasa, their home now filled with laughter and love. Their story is celebrated in festivals like Maha Shivratri, reminding us that devotion and patience can conquer any heart.

This tale of Shiva and Parvati is a love song, sweet and eternal. It makes me believe that love, when true, finds its way, like a river reaching the sea.

And so, Shiva and Parvati were united, a story of devotion, patience, and timeless love. From the Shiva Purana, this tale is cherished in temples and homes, especially during Maha Shivratri. It reminds me that love, when rooted in faith, can overcome any obstacle. Parvati's devotion and Shiva's awakening teach us that the heart's truest desires are worth waiting for. Whenever I see an image of Shiva and Parvati together, their serene smiles, I feel their love, whispering that every journey end in joy.

Story 7: Rama and Sita

The names Rama and Sita bring a serene calm to my heart, like the first ray of dawn soothing a weary soul. Their story, rooted in Valmiki's Ramayana, isn't just about a prince and princess—it's a saga of love, duty, and sacrifice that resonates in every heart. Rama, known as Maryada Purushottam—the ideal man—and Sita, the daughter of Mother Earth, were made for each other. Yet, their path was strewn with thorns. This story always reminds me that true love and righteousness may demand great trials, but they always triumph. Let's journey to the city of Ayodhya, where a prince's birth and his love story were destined to light the world's path.

Ayodhya was a city that seemed like a piece of heaven on earth. Nestled along the banks of the Sarayu River, its palaces shimmered with gold and silver, and its streets buzzed with the laughter of contented people. King Dasharatha, a proud ruler of the Ikshvaku dynasty, was beloved for his just governance. Yet, within his grand palace, a quiet sorrow lingered—he had no heir. Dasharatha and his three queens—Kaushalya, Sumitra, and Kaikeyi—spent years praying for a child, their hearts heavy with longing. I can feel their pain—a king with everything, yet his soul incomplete without the laughter of a child.

Finally, Dasharatha, guided by Sage Rishyashringa, performed the grand Putrakameshti Yagna. From the sacrificial fire emerged a divine figure, holding a golden vessel filled with celestial porridge. "Share this among your queens," he said. "You will be blessed with sons." Dasharatha's eyes welled with tears of joy. He divided the porridge among Kaushalya, Sumitra, and Kaikeyi. In time, Kaushalya gave birth to Rama, Kaikeyi to Bharata, and Sumitra to Lakshmana and Shatrughna. Ayodhya erupted in celebration—lamps were lit, flowers adorned the river, and sweets were shared. I imagine the city glowing, as if the stars had descended to rejoice.

Rama was special from childhood, like a fragment of the sun walking the earth. His smile brought peace to every heart, and his eyes held a deep tranquility. I picture him—a young prince, bow and arrow in hand, racing through Ayodhya's gardens with his brothers, their laughter echoing in the air. But Rama was more than a prince; he carried the weight of dharma on his shoulders. Sage Vashishta taught him the Vedas, scriptures, and martial arts. Rama obeyed every command with grace, his actions reflecting perfect righteousness. Yet, there was a tenderness in him, a softness that would later shine in his love for Sita.

As Rama grew into a young man, his fame spread far and wide. One day, Sage Vishvamitra arrived in Ayodhya, his face etched with concern. "Dasharatha," he said, "I need Rama and Lakshmana. Demons are destroying my ashram." Dasharatha's heart trembled. His beloved sons, so young, facing battle? I feel his anguish—a father desperate to shield his children from danger. But Rama stepped forward, gently touching his father's hand. "Father, this is my duty," he said calmly. His voice carried such strength that Dasharatha relented. Rama and Lakshmana set off with Vishvamitra into the forest.

In the jungle, Rama defeated the demoness Tadaka and her son Subahu, protecting the sages' hermitage. Vishvamitra gifted them divine weapons and mantras. But this journey was not just about battles. Vishvamitra led Rama to Mithila, where King Janaka's daughter Sita's swayamvara was being held. Mithila's streets were adorned with flowers, and the air rang with auspicious songs. Janaka possessed an ancient bow—Lord Shiva's, so heavy no one could lift it. The swayamvara's condition was clear: whoever could lift and string the bow would win Sita's hand.

The royal court was filled with princes, each trying and failing to move the bow. I see the scene—princes stepping back in defeat, Janaka's face clouded with disappointment. Then Vishvamitra nodded to Rama. Rama approached; his steps calm yet resolute. He gazed at the bow, as if greeting an old friend. With a deep breath, he lifted it effortlessly. The court held its breath. Then, with a resounding crack, Rama strung the bow—and it snapped, like thunder splitting the sky.

The court erupted in cheers. Sita, standing behind a curtain, stepped forward. In her hands was a garland, her face glowing with shy joy. I feel that moment—Rama and Sita's eyes meeting, as if two souls, separated for lifetimes, had finally reunited. Sita placed the garland around Rama's neck, and Mithila rejoiced. Janaka's eyes were moist, and Vishvamitra smiled knowingly. Dasharatha was summoned, and Ayodhya's royal entourage arrived. Rama and Sita's wedding was a dreamlike festival. I see them—Rama and Sita circling the sacred fire, petals raining from the heavens, and joyous songs filling the air. Lakshmana, Bharata, and Shatrughna married Sita's sisters—Urmila, Mandavi, and Shrutakirti.

But the true test of Rama and Sita's story lay ahead. Back in Ayodhya, as plans to crown Rama as heir began, Kaikeyi's maid Manthara sowed seeds of greed and envy. "Make Bharata king," she whispered. Kaikeyi, who once loved Rama like a son, was swayed. She demanded her two boons from Dasharatha—Bharata's coronation and Rama's exile for fourteen years. Dasharatha's heart shattered. I feel his agony—a king who dreamed of seeing his son on the throne, now forced to banish him. His eyes brimmed with tears, his body trembling with grief. Rama heard the news, but his face showed no trace of resentment. "My father's command is my dharma," he said. His voice held a calm that steadied even the storm around him. Sita took Rama's hand. "I cannot live without you," she said, her eyes shining with love and resolve. I feel her devotion—a queen ready to trade palace comforts for the hardships of the forest, all for Rama. Lakshmana joined them, saying, "My life is incomplete without my brother." The streets of Ayodhya wept as Rama, Sita, and Lakshmana, dressed in simple bark, walked toward the forest, leaving a grieving city behind. I see them—three figures, resolute, fading into the wilderness.

In the forest, Rama, Sita, and Lakshmana built a humble hut. Sita, raised in Mithila's palaces, now gathered fruits and cooked for Rama with joy. I see her simplicity—Sita smiling at Rama, as if the forest were her paradise. Rama protected sages, slaying demons who troubled them. But the greatest challenge came when Ravana, the demon king of Lanka, set his eyes on Sita. Ravana disguised himself as a golden deer, which Sita, enchanted, asked Rama to capture. Rama went, but it was a trap. Ravana abducted Sita, carrying her to Lanka.

When Rama returned and found Sita gone, his heart broke. I feel his pain—Rama, always composed, now incomplete without his beloved, his voice trembling as he called, "Sita, where are you?" Lakshmana consoled him, and they began their search. Along the way, they befriended Sugriva and Hanuman. Hanuman, Rama's greatest devotee, crossed the ocean to find Sita in Lanka. I see Hanuman's devotion—soaring over waves, delivering Rama's message to Sita, giving her hope.

Rama rallied a monkey army. I envision the scene—Rama, bow in hand, standing with Sugriva and Hanuman, marching toward Lanka. The ocean parted, and the army attacked. The war was fierce. Ravana's son Meghnada and brother Kumbhakarna challenged the monkeys. But Rama's bow thundered. I hear the clash—arrows whistling, Hanuman's roars, and Sita's prayers for Rama's victory. Finally, Rama slew Ravana, ending evil's reign.

Sita returned, but questions about her purity arose. I feel her pain—a devoted wife, who endured so much, yet faced scrutiny. Sita underwent the fire ordeal, and the flames testified to her purity. Rama and Sita returned to Ayodhya. I see that night—Diwali, when Ayodhya welcomed them with lamps, as if stars had descended. People sang, "Rama has come, Sita has come!"

Rama and Sita's story is a beacon of love and duty. It teaches me that true love demands sacrifice, and the path of righteousness is hard but victorious. Rama's calm, Sita's devotion, and their love's depth live in my heart, like the Sarayu's waves that never cease.

And so, the story of Rama and Sita lights the path of love, duty, and sacrifice. Drawn from Valmiki's Ramayana, it resounds in every temple and home, especially during Diwali. It reminds me that even on the toughest roads, love and faith lead to victory. Rama's bow and Sita's devotion dwell in our hearts, teaching us that truth and love never surrender. Whenever I see lamps glowing on Diwali night, I feel Rama and Sita's smiles blessing us still.

Story 8: Savitri and Satyavan

The story of Savitri and Satyavan feels like a poem, each word painted with love and devotion. Found in the Mahabharata's Vana Parva, it's the tale of a wife who wrested her husband back from the god of death. Savitri's courage and love shake my heart every time, teaching me that true love can conquer even death. This story always reminds me that a woman's strength lies in her devotion and wisdom. Let's travel to a time when a princess's love story moved the heavens.

Savitri, princess of Madra, was born a miracle. Her father, King Ashwapati, had performed years of penance, and Savitri was the fruit of his prayers. She wasn't just beautiful; her heart overflowed with compassion, and her wisdom left people in awe. I imagine her—Savitri, standing in her palace garden among blooming flowers, like a goddess descended to earth. But Savitri's mind was unique. She understood the world's sorrows, as if her heart was tied to every living being.

When Savitri reached marriageable age, Ashwapati said, "Daughter, choose your husband." Savitri obeyed, setting out to travel the kingdoms. I see her—Savitri, in simple attire, riding her chariot, searching for something in every prince's face. But none touched her heart. One day, she reached a dense forest where Satyavan lived. Satyavan was an exiled prince. His father, King

Dyumatsena, had lost his kingdom and now lived with his blind wife in a modest hut. Satyavan chopped wood, gathered fruits, and cared for his parents.

Savitri saw Satyavan. He was felling a tree, his arms strong, his face radiant with simplicity. I feel that moment—Savitri's eyes pausing on Satyavan, her heart whispering, "This is my companion." Satyavan looked at her, his eyes kind and gentle. Savitri decided, "I will marry Satyavan." She returned to her father and said, "Father, I have chosen Satyavan."

But then Sage Narada, who was present, warned her. "Savitri, Satyavan is noble, but he has only one year to live." Ashwapati's face paled. "Choose another," he urged. But Savitri's face was calm. "My choice is made," she said. "My love is greater than time." I salute her courage—a young woman, steadfast in her love despite knowing death's shadow. Ashwapati bowed his head, and Savitri's marriage to Satyavan was fixed.

The wedding was simple, held in the forest. Savitri shed her royal robes and moved to Satyavan's hut. I see her—Savitri, cooking for Satyavan, serving his parents, content in every moment. She went with Satyavan to the forest, helping him gather wood, laughing and talking. But every night, when all slept, Savitri prayed silently. "O God, save my Satyavan," she whispered, her eyes moist with tears. I feel her devotion—a wife fighting for her husband's life with every breath.

The foretold day arrived. Satyavan was chopping wood, Savitri by his side, counting his every breath. Suddenly, he grew dizzy and collapsed. Savitri laid him under a tree, his head in her lap. I see her pain—Savitri, watching her husband's breaths slow, yet her face serene. Then, Yama, the god of death, appeared, his eyes solemn, a noose in hand. "Savitri, Satyavan's time is up," he said. Savitri bowed but followed Yama as he took Satyavan's soul. "I cannot live without my husband," she said. Yama sternly replied, "Return, this is nature's law." But Savitri didn't stop. I see her courage—crossing forests, rivers, and mountains behind Yama, her love stronger than death's path. Savitri spoke, "You uphold dharma. Don't you understand a wife's duty?" Yama paused, his eyes turning to her.

With wisdom and devotion, Savitri reasoned with Yama. "Love is life," she said. "Satyavan is my foundation." Yama was moved. "You've won me, Savitri," he said. "Ask for anything but Satyavan's life." Savitri cleverly said, "Restore my father-in-law's kingdom, give him his sight, and bless me with a hundred sons." Yama granted all. But Savitri added, "I am a devoted wife. Without Satyavan, how can I be a mother?" Yama smiled. "You've outwitted me," he said. "Take Satyavan."

Savitri returned, and Satyavan's eyes opened. I feel that joy—Savitri embracing her husband, as if she'd conquered the world. They returned to their hut, and soon Dyumatsena's kingdom and sight were restored. Savitri and Satyavan lived happily, their story immortal. This tale is of a wife's love and courage. It teaches me that true love can bend even death. Savitri's devotion lights a lamp in my heart, whispering that love holds the power to make the impossible possible.

And so, Savitri won Satyavan back from Yama, a story of devotion, love, and courage. Drawn from the Mahabharata, it echoes during every Savitri-Satyavan Vrat. It reminds me that true love breaks all boundaries. Savitri's wisdom and faith inspire us, teaching that love has the strength to defeat death. Whenever I hear Savitri's story, I feel her courage burning within me.

Story 9: Krishna's Childhood Leelas

The name Krishna brings a smile to my lips and a flutter to my heart, like the sound of a flute floating over a quiet river. His childhood leelas, found in the Bhagavata Purana, are not just stories—they're bursts of divine joy, love, and mischief that make the world feel lighter. Krishna, the eighth avatar of Vishnu, came to earth to spread love and slay evil, but in Vrindavan, he was simply Kanha, the butter-thief, the darling of every heart. This story always reminds me that God's love is playful, close, and boundless, like a child's laughter. Let's wander to the lanes of Vrindavan, where a dark-skinned boy with a peacock feather stole hearts and worked miracles.

In the land of Braj, where the Yamuna River flowed like a silver ribbon, lay the village of Gokul. Its mud houses were humble, its fields green, and its air filled with the lowing of cows and the jingle of their bells. But Gokul's true treasure was its people—simple cowherds whose hearts were pure as the milk they churned. Among them lived Nanda and Yashoda, a couple whose love for each other was matched only by their longing for a child. I can feel their quiet ache—years of prayers, their home silent without a baby's giggle.

One stormy night, as rain lashed the earth and thunder roared, a miracle happened in Mathura, not far from Gokul. Devaki, imprisoned by her cruel brother Kamsa, gave birth to her eighth child—Krishna, the divine incarnation of Vishnu. Kamsa, warned by a prophecy that this child would kill him, had slain Devaki's previous babies. But that night, divine magic unfolded. The prison guards fell asleep, chains melted, and doors swung open. Vasudeva, Krishna's father, carried the newborn across the raging Yamuna, shielded by the serpent Sheshnaga's hoods. I see that scene—Vasudeva clutching tiny Krishna, the river parting, and the stars peeking through clouds to bless the child.

Vasudeva reached Gokul and swapped Krishna with Yashoda's newborn daughter, who was taken back to Mathura. Kamsa, thinking the girl was the prophesied child, tried to kill her, but she vanished, revealing herself as Goddess Durga and warning him of his doom. Meanwhile, in Gokul, Yashoda awoke to find a baby boy beside her, his skin dark as a monsoon cloud, his eyes twinkling like stars. She named him Krishna, meaning "the dark one," and her heart swelled with love. I imagine her cradling him, her face glowing, unaware that she held God himself.

Krishna's childhood was a whirlwind of mischief and miracles. From the moment he could crawl, he was unstoppable. His tiny hands reached for butter pots, his giggles filled the house, and his antics kept Yashoda on her toes. I see little Kanha, his face smeared with curd, toddling through Gokul's lanes, trailed by his friends—Balarama, Sudama, and others. The gopis, Gokul's milkmaids, adored him but pretended to scold. "Kanha, you stole my butter again!" they'd say, shaking their heads, but their eyes sparkled with love. Krishna would flash his dimpled smile, and their mock anger melted. I feel that warmth—his charm wrapping everyone in joy.

But Krishna's leelas weren't just playful; they were divine. One day, a demoness named Putana, sent by Kamsa, came to Gokul disguised as a beautiful woman. She offered to nurse Krishna, her milk laced with poison. Yashoda, trusting her, handed over her baby. Krishna latched on, but instead of dying, he sucked out Putana's life force, revealing her monstrous form. Yashoda screamed, running to snatch Krishna, but he lay in her arms, cooing happily. I feel her terror and relief—her baby safe, yet touched by something beyond her understanding.

Another time, a demon named Trinavarta came as a whirlwind, snatching Krishna into the sky. Gokul's women wailed, dust blinding their eyes. But Krishna, giggling, grew heavy, dragging Trinavarta down until the demon crashed and died. Krishna landed softly, clapping his hands as if it were a game. I see Yashoda, tears streaming, hugging him tight, her heart pounding with love and fear. "What are you, my Kanha?" she whispered, but Krishna only smiled, his eyes hiding the universe.

Krishna's love for butter earned him the name Makhan Chor—butter thief. He'd sneak into gopis' homes, climbing pots, breaking jars, and sharing the loot with his friends. One day, the gopis, fed up, tied him to a mortar as punishment. I see little Krishna, his wrists bound, looking at Yashoda with mock sorrow. But then he tugged the mortar, dragging it between two massive trees, uprooting them. From the trees emerged two celestial beings, freed from a curse by Krishna's touch. The gopis gasped, realizing their Kanha was no ordinary child. I feel their awe—loving him as a naughty boy, yet sensing his divinity.

As Krishna grew, his flute became his voice. He'd play it by the Yamuna, notes so sweet that cows stopped grazing, birds fell silent, and gopis forgot their chores. I hear that melody—soft, haunting, pulling hearts toward him. The gopis danced with him in the moonlight, their Raas Leela a divine celebration of love. Each felt Krishna danced with her alone, his love infinite. I feel their ecstasy—ordinary women touched by God's grace, their souls soaring.

Kamsa, meanwhile, sent demon after demon—Bakasura, Aghasura, Kaliya—but Krishna defeated them all. When Kaliya poisoned the Yamuna, Krishna danced on his hoods, taming him with grace. I see that dance—Krishna's feet twinkling, the serpent humbled, and Gokul's waters pure again. The cowherds watched, their hearts swelling with pride and wonder. "Our Kanha is special," they whispered, their love deepening.

One day, Krishna saw the cowherds preparing a sacrifice for Indra, the rain god. "Worship Govardhan Hill instead," he said. "It gives us food and shelter." The cowherds obeyed, and Indra, furious, unleashed torrential rains. Gokul flooded, people trembling in fear. But Krishna, just a boy, lifted Govardhan Hill on his little finger, sheltering everyone beneath it for seven days. I see that miracle—Krishna standing tall, the hill like an umbrella, and Gokul's people safe, singing his praises. Indra, humbled, bowed to Krishna, calling him Govinda, protector of cows.

Krishna's leelas were endless—each a lesson in love, courage, and faith. When he left Gokul for Mathura to face Kamsa, the gopis wept, their hearts breaking. I feel their pain—losing their Kanha, yet knowing his love would never fade. Krishna killed Kamsa, fulfilling his destiny, but his childhood in Vrindavan remained a golden memory, sung by devotees forever.

This story of Krishna's leelas is a river of joy, flowing with divine love. It teaches me that God is not distant but close, playful, and part of our lives. Krishna's flute, his mischief, and his miracles live in my heart, like a melody that never stops.

And so, Krishna's childhood leelas fill our hearts with divine joy, love, and wonder. From the Bhagavata Purana, these tales are sung in temples and homes, especially during Janmashtami. They remind me that God's love is playful and boundless, always near. Krishna's butter-stealing, flute-playing, and demon-slaying antics teach us that faith and love conquer all. Whenever I hear a flute's notes or see a peacock feather, I feel Krishna's mischievous smile, whispering that he's still dancing in our hearts.

Story 10: Draupadi's Swayamvara and Marriage

Draupadi's story stirs my soul like a fierce wind, carrying courage, destiny, and love. Found in the Mahabharata's Adi Parva, it's the tale of a princess born of fire, whose life intertwined with five legendary brothers—the Pandavas. Her swayamvara and marriage are not just about a royal wedding but a saga of strength, faith, and bonds that shaped an epic. Draupadi, also called Panchali, was no ordinary woman; she was a flame, fierce yet radiant with grace. This story always reminds me that destiny weaves complex paths, but love and courage light the way. Let's travel to Kampilya, where a princess's choice sparked a journey that changed the world.

In the kingdom of Panchala, ruled by King Drupada, the air was thick with ambition and prayer. Drupada, a proud warrior, had once been humiliated by his childhood friend Drona, who demanded half his kingdom as guru-dakshina. Burning with revenge, Drupada sought a son to defeat Drona. He performed a grand yagna, and from the sacrificial fire emerged two divine children—a son, Dhrishtadyumna, and a daughter, Draupadi. Draupadi was no ordinary princess. Her skin glowed like polished ebony, her eyes blazed with intelligence, and her presence commanded awe. I see her—Draupadi, born of flames, standing tall, her heart a mix of fire and grace. They called her Panchali, the pride of Panchala.

Draupadi grew into a woman of unmatched beauty and wisdom. Her laughter filled Drupada's palace, but her mind was sharp, her words piercing. I imagine her in Panchala's gardens, debating with scholars or practicing archery, her spirit as free as the wind. Drupada, seeing her radiance, decided it was time for her swayamvara. He wanted a husband worthy of his fiery daughter, someone who could match her strength and honor. Invitations were sent across Bharatvarsha, and Kampilya buzzed with preparations. I hear the excitement—drums beating, streets adorned with flowers, and whispers of the mysterious challenge awaiting the suitors.

Drupada devised a test to ensure only the greatest warrior could win Draupadi. A massive bow, heavier than any man could lift, was placed in the swayamvara hall. Above it hung a rotating fish, visible only in a pool of oil below. The suitor had to string the bow and shoot an arrow through the fish's eye, guided by its reflection. I feel the weight of that challenge—near impossible, designed to find a hero among men. Kings and princes arrived, their egos as grand as their armies. Karna, Duryodhana, Shishupala, and others filled the hall, each boasting of their prowess. I see Drupada, watching keenly, hoping for a worthy match for his daughter.

Meanwhile, in a forest far away, the Pandavas—five brothers born of divine blessings—lived in exile. Yudhishthira, Bhima,

Arjuna, Nakula, and Sahadeva, sons of Pandu, had lost their kingdom to a cruel twist of fate. Disguised as Brahmins, they wandered, their mother Kunti their guiding light. Arjuna, the third brother, was an archer unmatched, his focus as steady as a mountain. Hearing of Draupadi's swayamvara, Kunti urged her sons to attend, sensing destiny's call. I feel their resolve—the Pandavas, ragged yet regal, walking to Kampilya, their hearts heavy but hopeful.

The swayamvara day dawned, Kampilya glittering like a jewel. The hall was a sea of royalty, banners fluttering, and the air thick with anticipation. Draupadi entered, her crimson sari shimmering, a garland in her hands. I see her—tall, radiant, her eyes scanning the suitors, searching for someone worthy. One by one, the princes tried the bow. Kings strained, their faces red, but the bow wouldn't budge. Karna, the warrior of Anga, stepped forward. He lifted the bow with ease, and the crowd gasped. But Draupadi's voice rang out, firm and clear. "I will not marry a charioteer's son," she said, her pride unyielding. Karna's eyes darkened, and he stepped back, the bow untouched. I feel his pain—a warrior humiliated, yet bound by her choice.

The hall fell silent, the challenge unmet. Then, from the crowd, a young Brahmin rose—Arjuna, disguised in simple robes. Laughter rippled through the kings; a Brahmin daring to compete? But Arjuna's eyes were calm, his steps sure. I see him—Arjuna, bowing to the bow, his hands steady. He lifted it effortlessly, strung it, and gazed into the oil's reflection. With a single arrow, he pierced the fish's eye, the hall erupting in cheers. Draupadi's eyes met his, and she placed the garland around his neck. I feel that moment—two souls connected, destiny unfolding.

But the kings, enraged at a Brahmin's victory, attacked. Bhima and Arjuna fought back, their strength divine. The Pandavas escaped with Draupadi, returning to their hut. Kunti, unaware of the events, called from inside, "Share whatever you've brought equally." The brothers froze, Draupadi's heart pounding. Yudhishthira, bound by their vow to obey Kunti, declared Draupadi would marry all five. I feel the weight of that moment—Draupadi, a princess, facing an unimaginable fate, yet her courage unwavering.

Drupada, shocked at the news, summoned the Pandavas. Sage Vyasa appeared, revealing their true identities and explaining Draupadi's destiny—she was born to unite the Pandavas, her five husbands from a past life reborn. Draupada consented, and the weddings were held, each brother marrying Draupadi in a sacred ceremony. I see the fire—Draupadi circling it five times, her heart accepting her unique role. The Pandavas vowed to protect her, their bond sealed by love and duty.

Draupadi's marriage was no ordinary union; it was a partnership of equals. She became their strength, guiding them through exile, war, and triumph. Her courage in the face of trials—Duryodhana's insults, the dice game, her disrobing—ignited the Mahabharata's war. I feel her fire—Draupadi, a queen who stood tall, her love for her husbands and faith in Krishna her shield.

This story of Draupadi's swayamvara and marriage is a tapestry of courage, love, and destiny. It teaches me that true bonds withstand any test, and a woman's strength can shape history. Draupadi's fire and the Pandavas' devotion live in my heart, like a flame that never dims.

And so, Draupadi's swayamvara and marriage wove a bond that shaped an epic, a story of courage, love, and destiny. From the Mahabharata, it resonates in every retelling, inspiring hearts. It reminds me that love and strength conquer all trials. Draupadi's fire and the Pandavas' devotion teach us that destiny's paths, though complex, lead to truth. Whenever I hear of Draupadi, I feel her strength, whispering that love and courage can change the world.

Story 11: Vamana Avatar and Bali's Sacrifice

The story of Vamana Avatar and King Bali fills my heart with a quiet reverence, like the calm before a sacred ritual. Found in the Bhagavata Purana, it's a tale of Lord Vishnu's fifth incarnation and a demon king's extraordinary generosity that shook the heavens. Bali, an asura king of immense power, and Vamana, a diminutive Brahmin who was Vishnu himself, are the heroes of this saga. This story always teaches me that true devotion and selflessness can dissolve pride, and God never ignores a devotee's call. Let's travel to a time when a tiny Brahmin measured the universe in three steps, and a king's sacrifice became immortal.

Long ago, when the world was young, the demon king Bali ruled over the three realms—earth, heaven, and the netherworld. Bali, grandson of the devout Prahlada and son of Virochana, inherited his forefather's faith but was driven by ambition. Through rigorous penance and unmatched valor, he defeated the gods and seized control of heaven. I see that scene—Indra's golden palace in heaven, now empty, and Bali, seated on the throne, surrounded by his fierce asura warriors, his face glowing with triumph. Yet, Bali was no ordinary demon. His heart was generous, his rule just, and his devotion sincere. He cared for his subjects, performed grand sacrifices, and showered Brahmins with gifts. I feel his nobility—a demon king whose soul pulsed with devotion, despite his pride.

The gods, dethroned and desperate, approached Lord Vishnu in Vaikuntha. "O Lord," Indra pleaded, "Bali has taken heaven. Save us!" Vishnu, reclining on Sheshnaga, smiled gently. "Bali is my devotee," he said. "But for the sake of dharma, I will restore balance." I sense Vishnu's compassion—a God who honored his devotee yet acted to protect the cosmos. Vishnu took the form of Vamana, a tiny Brahmin boy, no taller than a child, with a serene face and eyes that held the depth of the universe. Clad in a simple loincloth, holding a water pot and an umbrella, Vamana descended to earth. I see him—Vamana, his small steps light, like a spark of divinity walking among mortals.

Meanwhile, Bali was performing a grand Ashwamedha Yagna on the banks of the Narmada. His sacrificial pavilion glittered with gold, Vedic chants filled the air, and Brahmins thronged to receive his gifts. Bali's guru, Shukracharya, stood by his side, guiding him with wisdom. I envision that spectacle—the sacrificial fire blazing, the scent of ghee wafting, and Bali, in regal attire, distributing wealth with a proud yet devout heart. Suddenly, a small Brahmin appeared at the gate—Vamana. His simplicity amused the guards, but Bali, sensing something divine, rose to welcome him. "O Brahmin, what do you seek?" he asked, his voice warm with respect.

Vamana's voice was calm, like a gentle breeze. "O King, I ask for just three paces of land, measured by my steps." I feel the simplicity of that moment—Vamana, with his modest request, and Bali, astonished that such a great king was asked for so little. Bali laughed heartily. "Young Brahmin, why so little? I can give you jewels, gold, entire villages!" But Vamana shook his head. "Three paces will suffice." Shukracharya's eyes narrowed. "Beware, O King," he whispered. "This is no ordinary Brahmin. He may be Vishnu himself." I see Shukracharya's concern—a guru desperate to protect his disciple from a divine trap.

But Bali's heart was resolute. "Gurudev," he said, "I have given my word. If this is Lord Vishnu, I am blessed to offer him my all." I salute Bali's devotion—a demon king who placed his promise and faith above his ego. Bali took the vow to grant the gift, and Vamana smiled. Then, a miracle unfolded. Vamana's tiny form began to grow. He became colossal, his head touching the heavens, his feet reaching the netherworld. I see that awe-inspiring sight—Vamana, now Trivikrama, a cosmic giant whose presence dwarfed the universe.

With his first step, Vamana covered the entire earth. With his second, he encompassed heaven. Bali's court stood frozen, their breath caught in wonder. Vamana's voice echoed, "O King, where shall I place my third step?" Bali, his pride shattered, bowed low. "O Lord," he said, "I have nothing left. Place your foot on my head." I feel the depth of that surrender—Bali, offering his very self, his devotion shining brighter than his crown. Vamana placed his foot on Bali's head, gently pressing him to Patala, the netherworld.

Yet Vishnu's heart melted at Bali's selflessness. "Bali, you are my true devotee," he said. "I grant you sovereignty over Patala and immortality. One day, you shall become Indra." I see Vishnu's mercy—a God who, even in Bali's defeat, ensured his glory. The gods reclaimed heaven, and Bali descended to Patala, but his sacrifice became eternal. Legends say Bali returns to earth each year, celebrated in Kerala's Onam festival, where homes bloom with flowers to welcome their beloved king. I envision that joy—flower carpets, boat races, and songs of Bali's devotion ringing through the air.

This story is one of devotion, humility, and sacrifice. It teaches me that true generosity transcends ego, and God hears every devotee's call. Bali's vow and Vamana's grace live in my heart, like a river that never stops flowing.

And so, the story of Vamana Avatar and Bali's sacrifice lights the path of devotion, humility, and generosity. Drawn from the Bhagavata Purana, it resonates in homes and temples, especially during Onam. It reminds me that a true devotee's faith makes them immortal. Bali's sacrifice and Vamana's compassion inspire us, teaching that God never forsakes his devotee. Whenever I see Onam's floral patterns, I feel Bali's devotion blessing us still.

Story 12: Markandeya and Shiva's Boon

The tale of Markandeya and Shiva's boon is like a sacred melody, singing of devotion and triumph over death. Found in the Shiva Purana, it's the story of a young sage's unwavering faith and Lord Shiva's boundless grace. Markandeya, a mere boy who faced death with courage, and Shiva, who came to save his devotee, are its heart. This story always teaches me that true faith can conquer even death, and Shiva never turns away from a devotee's cry. Let's journey to a time when a child's devotion shook the god of death, and Mahadev granted the boon of immortality.

In ancient times, in a tranquil forest, lived the sage Mrikandu and his wife, Marudvati. Mrikandu, a learned scholar and ardent Shiva devotee, was revered for his wisdom and penance. Yet, a quiet sorrow lingered in their lives—they had no child. I feel their pain—a sage with a treasury of knowledge, yet an ashram silent without a child's laughter. Mrikandu and Marudvati undertook severe penance, chanting "Om Namah Shivaya" day and night, their hearts yearning for a son.

Shiva, the compassionate destroyer, appeared before them. "Mrikandu, I am pleased with your devotion," he said. "But you must choose: a hundred foolish sons who live long, or one wise and devout son who lives only sixteen years." Mrikandu and Marudvati exchanged glances, and Mrikandu replied, "O Lord, give us one wise and devout son, even if his life is short." I admire their selflessness—parents who valued their child's virtue over longevity.

Shiva smiled, and soon Marudvati gave birth to a son, named Markandeya, meaning "the victorious." Markandeya was extraordinary from birth. His eyes were deep, as if holding the wisdom of ages, and his face radiated peace. I see him—little Markandeya in his father's ashram, reciting Vedas, worshipping the Shivalinga, his heart immersed in devotion. Mrikandu taught him scriptures, yoga, and Shiva-bhakti. But as Markandeya grew, a shadow crept over his parents' faces. I feel their anguish—they knew their son's life would end at sixteen.

When Markandeya learned of his short lifespan, his face remained serene. "Father, Mother, do not worry," he said. "Lord Shiva is with me." I salute his courage—a boy facing death's shadow with unshakable faith. Markandeya deepened his devotion, spending hours by the river, crafting a Shivalinga from clay, offering flowers, and chanting "Om Namah Shivaya." His devotion was so pure that birds fell silent, and the air shimmered with sanctity. I see that scene—Markandeya, eyes closed, lost in Shiva, his soul soaring to Kailasa.

The fateful day arrived when Markandeya turned sixteen. Yama, the god of death, came with his noose to claim him. Markandeya was worshipping the Shivalinga, his heart wholly surrendered to

Shiva. Yama cast his noose, but the Shivalinga deflected it. I feel the tension of that moment—Markandeya, absorbed in devotion, and Yama, stunned that his noose failed. Then, a thunderous roar shook the earth. From the Shivalinga emerged Lord Shiva, his eyes blazing with fury, his trident gleaming. "Yama, how dare you touch my devotee?" Shiva roared.

Yama trembled. "O Lord, it is nature's law," he said. "Markandeya's time is up." But Shiva's wrath was unyielding. "My devotee is beyond death," he declared. "Markandeya shall be immortal." I hear the echoes of that moment—Shiva's roar, Yama's submission, and Markandeya's prayers. Yama bowed and retreated. Shiva embraced Markandeya, like a father holding his son. "Markandeya, you are my true devotee," he said. "You shall live forever, and your name will be a beacon of devotion."

Markandeya's eyes brimmed with tears. "O Lord, I seek only your devotion," he said. I see his selflessness—a youth who, even with immortality, asked only to serve Shiva. Markandeya devoted his life to Shiva-bhakti and spreading wisdom, becoming a sage whose tales echo in the Puranas. Legends say Markandeya still roams, chanting Shiva's name. I feel his devotion—Markandeya, an eternal wanderer, his heart one with Shiva.

This story is of devotion and victory over death. It teaches me that true faith transcends all obstacles, and Shiva hears every devotee's call. Markandeya's devotion and Shiva's grace light a lamp in my heart, whispering that faith holds the power to defeat even death.

And so, the tale of Markandeya and Shiva's boon shows us the path of devotion, faith, and triumph over death. Drawn from the Shiva Purana, it resonates in temples and homes, especially during Shivaratri. It reminds me that a true devotee is never alone. Markandeya's faith and Shiva's compassion live in our hearts, teaching that God never ignores a devotee's cry. Whenever I offer water on a Shivalinga, I feel Markandeya's devotion echoing within me.

Story 13: Kurma Avatar and the Churning of the Ocean

The story of Kurma Avatar and the Churning of the Ocean fills my heart with wonder, like gazing at a starry sky that holds the universe's secrets. Found in the Bhagavata Purana, it's a tale of Lord Vishnu's second incarnation as a tortoise, guiding gods and demons in a cosmic quest for the nectar of immortality. This saga, distinct from the earlier Ocean Churning tale, centers on Vishnu's Kurma form, his wisdom, and the unity of opposites for a divine purpose. It always teaches me that even in chaos, divine grace brings balance, and cooperation can yield miracles. Let's journey to a time when the ocean was churned, gods and demons joined hands, and a tortoise held the world steady.

In the dawn of creation, when the world was still finding its rhythm, the gods (devas) and demons (asuras) were locked in endless rivalry. The gods, led by Indra, ruled heaven, their palaces gleaming with divine splendor. The demons, fierce and ambitious, sought to overthrow them. A curse from Sage Durvasa weakened the gods, stripping their strength and luster. I see that moment—Indra's throne dim, the gods weary, their faces etched with worry as the demons grew bolder. The heavens trembled, and the balance of the cosmos wavered. I feel their despair—divine beings, humbled, searching for hope.

The gods sought refuge at Lord Vishnu's abode in Vaikuntha. Reclining on Sheshnaga, Vishnu listened to their pleas. "O Lord," Indra said, "we are weak, and the demons threaten dharma. Save us!" Vishnu's eyes twinkled with wisdom. "Fear not," he said. "The nectar of immortality, Amrita, lies hidden in the Ocean of Milk. Churn the ocean to obtain it. But you must work with the demons, for this task requires both strength and unity." I sense Vishnu's foresight—a God who saw beyond rivalry, weaving a plan for cosmic harmony.

The gods, though hesitant, approached the demons, led by King Bali (before his Vamana encounter). Bali, a proud yet pragmatic leader, agreed to the alliance, lured by the promise of Amrita. I see that pact—gods and demons, sworn enemies, standing together on the shores of the milky ocean, its waves shimmering like liquid silver. To churn the ocean, they needed a churning rod and rope. Mount Mandara, a towering peak, was chosen as the rod, and Vasuki, the serpent king, offered himself as the rope. I envision that scene—Mandara's golden slopes gleaming, Vasuki's coils glistening, and the air buzzing with anticipation.

But as the gods and demons uprooted Mandara, its weight overwhelmed them. It began to sink into the ocean's depths. I feel their frustration—such a grand plan, faltering at the start. Then, Vishnu appeared as Kurma, a colossal tortoise, his shell vast as a mountain, his eyes calm yet profound. "I shall bear Mandara," Kurma said, diving beneath the ocean. He positioned himself under the mountain, his shell steady as the earth itself. I see Kurma—his mighty form, unyielding, holding the universe's hope on his back. The gods and demons cheered, their spirits renewed.

With Mandara balanced on Kurma's shell, the churning began. The gods held Vasuki's tail, the demons his head, and they pulled in rhythm, the ocean swirling into a frothy whirlpool. I hear that sound—waves crashing, Vasuki hissing, and Vedic chants echoing as Brahmins blessed the effort. But the churning was grueling. Vasuki, strained, spewed venom, burning the demons. The gods, at the tail, grew weary, their hands blistered. I feel their struggle—enemies forced to trust each other, united by a shared goal yet tested by pain.

As the ocean churned, treasures emerged. First came Kamadhenu, the wish-fulfilling cow, claimed by the sages. Then the Airavata elephant, taken by Indra. The Kaustubha gem adorned Vishnu's chest, and the Parijata tree perfumed heaven. I see these wonders—each gift sparkling, the gods and demons marveling, their rivalry forgotten in awe. But then, a dark cloud rose from the ocean—Kalakuta, a deadly poison that choked the air, threatening all creation. Panic gripped both sides. I feel that terror—the world on the brink, hope fading.

The gods and demons turned to Lord Shiva. Shiva, seated on Kailasa, sensed the crisis. With Parvati's gentle nod, he descended to the ocean. "I shall drink the poison," he said, his voice steady. He scooped the venom in his palms and swallowed it, his throat turning blue, earning him the name Neelkantha. I see Shiva—his serene face, the poison contained, his sacrifice saving the cosmos. The gods and demons bowed, their hearts filled with gratitude. I feel that moment—Shiva's selflessness, a beacon of divine love.

With the poison gone, the churning resumed, Kurma's shell unyielding beneath Mandara. Vasuki writhed, but Kurma's calm presence soothed him. Finally, Dhanvantari, the physician of the gods, emerged, holding a pot of Amrita. I see that golden moment—the nectar glowing, the gods and demons breathless with longing. But the demons, led by Rahu, seized the pot, unwilling to share. Vishnu, ever-watchful, took the form of Mohini, a celestial enchantress whose beauty captivated all. I envision Mohini—her grace disarming, her smile hiding divine intent.

Mohini charmed the demons, promising to distribute the nectar fairly. She seated gods and demons in rows, serving the gods first. Rahu, disguised as a god, sipped the nectar, but Surya and Chandra alerted Vishnu. Mohini severed Rahu's head, but his immortality made him Rahu-Ketu, celestial shadows forever chasing the sun and moon. I see that drama—Mohini's swift justice, the demons outwitted, and the gods restored with Amrita's power.

The churning complete, Kurma vanished into the ocean, his mission fulfilled. The gods reclaimed heaven, their strength renewed, and dharma was restored. The demons, though defeated, earned respect for their role. I feel the harmony of that outcome—enemies united, a cosmic balance achieved through Kurma's grace. The Ocean of Milk grew calm, its waves whispering tales of divine unity.

This story of Kurma Avatar is one of balance, sacrifice, and divine wisdom. It teaches me that even in conflict, cooperation and faith can yield miracles, and God's presence steadies every storm. Kurma's silent strength and Vishnu's guidance live in my heart, like a quiet anchor in life's ocean.

Ending

And so, the story of Kurma Avatar and the Churning of the Ocean shines as a beacon of divine wisdom and unity. From the Bhagavata Purana, it echoes in temples and festivals, reminding us of cosmic balance. It teaches me that faith and selflessness overcome chaos. Kurma's strength, Shiva's sacrifice, and Vishnu's grace inspire us, showing that God's love guides every endeavor. Whenever I see a tortoise, I feel Kurma's quiet power, steadying the world with devotion.

Story 14: Bhagiratha and the Descent of Ganga

The tale of Bhagiratha and the Descent of Ganga is like a sacred hymn, flowing with devotion, perseverance, and divine grace. Found in the Ramayana's Bala Kanda, it's the story of a king's relentless penance and the miraculous arrival of the Ganga River to earth. Bhagiratha, a mortal driven by duty to his ancestors, and Ganga, the celestial river goddess, are the soul of this saga. This story always reminds me that true devotion can move heavens, and God's compassion answers even the hardest prayers. Let's travel to a time when a king's tapasya brought the river of life to earth, redeeming souls and blessing humanity.

Long ago, in the lineage of King Ikshvaku, ruled the noble kings of Ayodhya. One such king, Sagara, was renowned for his valor and righteousness. Sagara had sixty thousand sons, each a mighty warrior, born to his queen Sumati, and one son, Anshumana, from his second queen, Keshini. I see Sagara's court—grand yet warm, filled with the pride of a father whose sons were his strength. Sagara desired to perform the Ashwamedha Yagna to proclaim his sovereignty, a ritual where a sacred horse roamed freely, guarded by his sons. I feel his ambition—a king seeking to unite the land under dharma.

The horse wandered across kingdoms, unchallenged, until it vanished near Sage Kapila's ashram. Sagara's sixty thousand sons, assuming treachery, stormed the hermitage, accusing Kapila of theft. Kapila, a sage of immense power, was deep in meditation. Disturbed, his eyes blazed with anger, reducing the sons to ashes with a single glance. I see that tragedy—Sagara's sons, proud warriors, now heaps of ash, their souls trapped, unliberated. Sagara, heartbroken, learned of their fate from Kapila's disciple. "Only the waters of Ganga can redeem their souls," the sage said. I feel Sagara's grief—a father mourning his sons, his heart heavy with duty.

Sagara passed his throne to Anshumana and spent his life in penance, praying for Ganga's descent, but he died without success. Anshumana, and later his son Dilipa, continued the penance, their lives dedicated to their ancestors' salvation. I see their resolve—kings trading royal comforts for austerity, their prayers echoing in the Himalayas. Yet, Ganga remained in heaven, flowing through Brahma's kamandalu, her waters too mighty for earth. I feel their longing—a lineage bound by love for their forefathers, yet unable to fulfill their vow.

Then came Bhagiratha, Dilipa's son, a king whose heart burned with duty. Bhagiratha was no ordinary ruler. His eyes held a quiet fire, his resolve unbreakable. I see him—Bhagiratha, standing in Ayodhya's palace, vowing to bring Ganga to earth. He entrusted his kingdom to his ministers and retreated to the Himalayas, clad in simple bark, his heart fixed on Brahma. Bhagiratha stood on one leg, arms raised, chanting Brahma's name, surviving on air alone. I feel his tapasya—the sun scorching, winters freezing, yet Bhagiratha unmoved, his soul soaring to the heavens.

Years passed, Bhagiratha's body frail but his spirit blazing. Brahma appeared, moved by his devotion. "Bhagiratha, I am pleased," he said. "Ganga will descend. But her force will shatter the earth. Only Shiva can bear her." I see Brahma's compassion—a creator granting a boon, yet guiding the path. Bhagiratha bowed, his heart now turned to Shiva. He trekked to Kailasa's foothills, crafting a Shivalinga, offering bilva leaves, and chanting "Om Namah Shivaya." I envision Bhagiratha—his voice trembling with devotion, his eyes fixed on Shiva, undeterred by hunger or cold.

Shiva, seated in meditation, felt Bhagiratha's pure heart. He appeared, his matted locks flowing, his trident gleaming. "I will hold Ganga," Shiva said, his voice like thunder. I see that divine moment—Shiva, standing tall, ready to tame a celestial river for a mortal's plea. Brahma released Ganga from his kamandalu, and she descended, her waters roaring like a thousand storms. Ganga, proud of her might, thought, "I'll sweep Shiva to Patala." But Shiva smiled, opening his matted locks. Ganga plunged in, her torrents lost in his hair, unable to flow out. I feel Ganga's humbling—her pride tamed, her waters trapped in Shiva's infinite locks.

Bhagiratha, watching, prayed fervently. "O Mahadev, release Ganga for my ancestors!" Shiva, moved by his devotion, let a single stream trickle from his locks, gentle yet pure. I see that sacred flow—Ganga, now calm, winding through the Himalayas, her waters sparkling like diamonds. Bhagiratha led Ganga across the plains, her path carving valleys and forests. I hear her song—Ganga's waves whispering blessings, nourishing the earth.

But Ganga's journey wasn't smooth. Near Sage Jahnu's ashram, her waters flooded his hermitage. Angered, Jahnu drank her up. Bhagiratha pleaded, "O Sage, my ancestors await salvation!" Jahnu, softened, released Ganga from his ear, earning her the name Jahnavi. I see that miracle—Ganga flowing again, Bhagiratha's faith unwavering. Finally, Ganga reached the ashes of Sagara's sons at Ganga Sagar. Her waters touched them, their souls rising to heaven, liberated at last. I feel that triumph—Bhagiratha, tears streaming, watching his ancestors ascend, his vow fulfilled.

Ganga became Bhagirathi, the river of Bhagiratha's penance, blessing humanity with her purity. I see her today—Ganga flowing through Haridwar, Varanasi, and beyond, her banks alive with prayers. Bhagiratha returned to Ayodhya, ruling as a sage-king, his life a testament to devotion.

This story is of perseverance, devotion, and divine grace. It teaches me that true faith can move mountains and rivers, and God answers the purest prayers. Bhagiratha's penance and Ganga's descent live in my heart, like a sacred river that never dries.

And so, the tale of Bhagiratha and the Descent of Ganga flows with devotion, sacrifice, and divine grace. From the Ramayana, it echoes in temples and ghats, especially during Ganga Dussehra. It reminds me that faith can achieve the impossible. Bhagiratha's resolve and Ganga's purity inspire us, teaching that God's compassion answers every sincere prayer. Whenever I see Ganga's waters, I feel Bhagiratha's devotion, blessing us still.

Story 15: Parashurama and the Kshatriya Purge

The story of Parashurama and the Kshatriya Purge sweeps my heart into a stormy wilderness, where the clash of duty, rage, and dharma roars like thunder. Found in the Mahabharata and Brahma Purana, this is the tale of Lord Vishnu's sixth incarnation, Parashurama, and his relentless war against tyrannical Kshatriyas. Parashurama, a Brahmin warrior whose axe was a symbol of justice, and his sacrifice for his parents, are the heart of this saga. This story always teaches me that even anger can be a tool for dharma when guided by righteousness, and its end lies in compassion and balance. Let's travel to a time when a Brahmin's axe cleansed the earth of Kshatriya oppression, and an avatar's wrath became eternal.

Long ago, when the earth was ruled by Kshatriya kings, the world was a mix of light and shadow. Some kings were just, upholding dharma, but many grew arrogant, their power turning to tyranny. They oppressed Brahmins, sages, and common folk, as if the light of righteousness had dimmed. I feel that darkness—ashrams looted, villagers trembling, and sages' prayers echoing to the heavens. In this era, in the Bhrigu clan, lived a Brahmin couple, Jamadagni and Renuka, in a humble ashram nestled in a lush forest. Jamadagni, a great sage, was renowned for his penance and wisdom, and Renuka, his devoted wife, stood by him in every ritual. I see their ashram—a haven of green, with cows grazing, a yagna fire glowing, like a slice of paradise.

Jamadagni and Renuka had five sons, the youngest named Rama, later known as Parashurama, "Rama with the axe." Rama was extraordinary from childhood. His eyes held a fiery calm, a blend of peace and power, and his heart was drawn to devotion and martial arts. I see him—young Rama, learning Vedas from his father, helping his mother, and practicing archery in the woods, his face alight with resolve. Lord Vishnu incarnated as Parashurama to rid the earth of Kshatriya tyranny. Lord Shiva gifted him an axe, which became his namesake—Parashurama, the axe-wielder. I feel that moment—Shiva's blessing, Parashurama's axe, as if a new warrior of dharma was forged.

Jamadagni owned Kamadhenu, a divine cow who fulfilled every wish, a treasure that fed the poor through his generosity. I picture Kamadhenu—her milky-white form, her gentle eyes radiating divinity, as if she were Lakshmi herself. But this cow caught the eye of Kartavirya Arjuna, also called Sahasrara, king of Hastinapura, a mighty ruler with a thousand arms, drowned in pride. His greed led him to Jamadagni's ashram with his army. "Sage, surrender this cow to my palace," he demanded, his voice dripping with arrogance. Jamadagni refused gently. "This cow is for the needy, O king." I salute his courage—a sage standing firm for truth against a king's might.

Kartavirya's pride erupted into rage. He ordered his soldiers to seize the cow, and they ravaged the ashram, dragging Kamadhenu away. I feel the devastation—the ashram in ruins, cows wailing, and Renuka's tears flowing. Jamadagni remained calm, but Parashurama, away in the forest, returned to see the chaos. His face blazed with anger. "Father, I will bring Kamala back," he vowed. I see his resolve—a son unable to bear his parents' dishonor. Parashurama, axe in hand, marched to Kartavirya's capital, Mahishmati.

A fierce battle ensued. Kartavirya's thousand arms were formidable, but Parashurama's axe was a whirlwind of justice. I envision the battlefield—Parashurama, a lone Brahmin, slicing through Kartavirya's army, his axe stained with blood. Finally, he felled Kartavirya, severing his arms, and rescued Kamadhenu. He returned the cow to the ashram, but the victory was bittersweet. Kartavirya's sons, fueled by vengeance, plotted retribution. One day, while Parashurama was away, they attacked the ashram and killed Jamadagni. I feel the tragedy—Jamadagni, a sage, slain in his sanctuary, Renuka screaming, their world shattered.

Parashurama returned to find his father's body. Renuka, preparing to join him as a sati, turned to her son. "End this tyranny, my child," she urged. Parashurama's heart broke, but his rage became a volcano. I see his anguish—a son who lost his father and watched his mother ascend into flames. He vowed, "I will rid the earth of oppressive Kshatriyas." Axe in hand, he launched a crusade that would echo through ages.

Parashurama circled the earth twenty-one times, challenging every tyrannical Kshatriya king. His axe carved rivers of blood, a storm of dharma cleansing the land. I hear the roar of those battles—Parashurama, solitary, facing armies, his axe a beacon of justice. Yet his wrath was not mere vengeance; it was dharma's defense. He spared righteous Kshatriyas, like Dasharatha and Janaka. I feel his compassion—a warrior who, even in fury, upheld righteousness.

When the earth was finally free of tyranny, Parashurama's anger subsided. He cast his axe into the sea, its blood forming coastal lands like the Konkan. I sense that closure—Parashurama, his mission complete, yet carrying his father's memory. He retired to the Himalayas for penance, but his legacy endured. In the Mahabharata, he mentored Bhishma and Karna, ever dharma's guardian. His story lives on, a testament to divine justice.

This story is of duty, righteousness, and righteous anger. It teaches me that a warrior's fury, when aligned with dharma, serves justice, and its end is compassion. Parashurama's axe and devotion kindle a fire in my heart, whispering that dharma always triumphs.

And so, the story of Parashurama and the Kshatriya Purge lights the path of duty, righteousness, and justice. Drawn from the Mahabharata and Brahma Purana, it resonates in temples, especially during Parashurama Jayanti. It reminds me that righteous anger can be sacred, purifying dharma. Parashurama's legacy and devotion live in our hearts, teaching that a true warrior fights for righteousness. Whenever I stand by the sea, I feel Parashurama's roar still echoing within.

Story 16: Ahalya's Redemption

The tale of Ahalya's Redemption is like a sacred prayer, whispering of sin, repentance, and divine mercy. Found in the Ramayana's Bala Kanda, it's the story of a holy woman, Ahalya, and the grace of Lord Rama that restored her. Ahalya, a sage's wife turned to stone by a curse, and Rama, who freed her, are the soul of this saga. This story always teaches me that true repentance washes away every sin, and God's compassion touches every heart. Let's journey to a time when a stone-bound soul found liberation, and Rama's mercy became eternal.

In the dawn of creation, when the world was fresh and pure, Brahma crafted a woman of unmatched beauty, wisdom, and sanctity—Ahalya. Ahalya was so radiant that even gods bowed before her. I see her—Ahalya, her eyes deep as oceans of knowledge, her face glowing with serenity. Brahma entrusted Ahalya to Sage Gautama, a revered ascetic. Their marriage was divine, and they lived in a tranquil ashram in a verdant forest. I picture their ashram—a sanctuary of green, with a river's murmur and a yagna's glow, like a corner of heaven.

Ahalya was Gautama's devoted wife, serving him with love and purity. She fetched water from the river at dawn, tended the ashram, and studied Vedas with him. I feel her devotion—a woman whose life was her husband and dharma. But Ahalya's beauty drew the gaze of Indra, king of the gods. Consumed by lust, Indra yearned to possess her. I see his weakness—a god blinded by desire, his divinity lost to pride.

One night, when Gautama was at the river for his ablutions, Indra took Gautama's form and approached Ahalya. In the darkness, Ahalya mistook him for her husband. But as Gautama returned, the truth dawned. I feel that heartbreak—Gautama, seeing his wife, his trust shattered, and Ahalya, stunned by her unwitting mistake. Gautama's fury flared. He cursed Indra, "Your body will bear the shame of a thousand eyes." Indra's form was marked forever, and he fled. But Gautama also cursed Ahalya. "You shall become stone until Lord Rama frees you." I see Ahalya's agony—a pure woman, trapped by circumstance, condemned to stone.

Ahalya turned to stone, her body a silent rock in the forest. Yet her soul lived, steeped in repentance and prayer. I feel her penance—Ahalya, locked in stone, chanting Rama's name, her spirit yearning for liberation. Years passed, ages turned, and Ahalya's stone was covered in dust. But her prayers reached the heavens. I see that quiet forest—birds singing, breezes whispering, and Ahalya's stone, a silent plea.

Centuries later, Lord Rama, accompanied by Sage Vishwamitra and his brother Lakshmana, passed through that forest en route to Mithila for Sita's swayamvara. Rama, Vishnu's incarnation, was guided by Vishwamitra, who knew Ahalya's tale. "Rama, this is Ahalya," he said, pointing to the stone. "Her time for redemption has come." I feel that moment—Rama, his eyes filled with compassion, gazing at the stone. Rama touched the stone with his foot, and a miracle unfolded. The rock cracked, and Ahalya emerged, her beauty and purity restored. I see that scene—Ahalya, at Rama's feet, her eyes brimming with tears, and Rama, smiling, like a father embracing his daughter.

Ahalya bowed to Rama. "O Lord, you have freed me," she said, her voice trembling. Rama replied, "Ahalya, your repentance has made you purer than before. Return to your husband." Gautama, deep in penance, saw Ahalya and softened. He embraced her, and they resumed their life in the ashram. I feel that reunion—Ahalya and Gautama, bound by love and forgiveness, their lives reborn.

Rama, Vishwamitra, and Lakshmana continued to Mithila, but Ahalya's redemption became immortal. Some say Ahalya's stone is still worshipped in temples, a testament to her devotion. I feel her faith—Ahalya, a soul that rose above sin, and Rama's grace, which revives every stone.

This story is of repentance, compassion, and liberation. It teaches me that true remorse cleanses every sin, and God's mercy reaches every soul. Ahalya's prayer and Rama's grace light a lamp in my heart, whispering that no soul is beyond redemption.

And so, the tale of Ahalya's Redemption shines with repentance, compassion, and divine mercy. Drawn from the Ramayana, it echoes in temples and homes, especially during Ram Navami. It reminds me that true faith breaks every curse. Ahalya's devotion and Rama's grace live in our hearts, teaching that God hears every prayer. Whenever I chant Rama's name, I feel Ahalya's redemption resonating within me.

Story 17: Matsya Avatar and the Great Flood

The story of Matsya Avatar and the Great Flood washes over my heart like a sacred river, carrying whispers of divine mercy, human faith, and the promise of renewal. Found in the Matsya Purana, this is the tale of Lord Vishnu's first incarnation as a fish, guiding humanity through a cataclysm to restore dharma. King Manu, a righteous soul chosen by destiny, and Matsya, a divine fish whose wisdom saved the world, are the heart of this saga. This story fills me with awe, teaching that even in the darkest deluge, God's compassion shines, and faith can rebuild a broken world. Let's journey to a time when the earth drowned in chaos, a fish led a king to salvation, and life bloomed anew.

In the dawn of creation, when the world was young and vibrant, the earth was a tapestry of forests, rivers, and kingdoms, ruled by righteous kings under dharma's light. But as yugas turned, greed and sin crept into human hearts, dimming the world's purity. I see that shadow—villages plundered, sages mocked, and rivers choked with neglect, as if the earth herself wept. The gods, watching from the heavens, grew heavy with concern. Brahma, the creator, foresaw a great flood that would cleanse the earth, washing away its sins to begin anew. I feel his resolve—a father ready to heal his creation, yet yearning to save the worthy.

In this era lived King Manu, a descendant of Swayambhu Manu, the first man. Manu was no ordinary king. His heart was a temple of dharma, his life devoted to his people and the gods. I see him—tall and gentle, his eyes deep with wisdom, his hands calloused from serving his kingdom. He ruled from a modest palace, rising before dawn to pray by the river, offering water to Surya, and tending to his subjects' needs. I feel his humility—a king who lived for others, his crown a symbol of duty, not pride. Manu's devotion caught Vishnu's eye, who chose him to preserve life through the coming deluge.

One morning, as Manu performed his ablutions by the Kritamala River, a tiny fish leapt into his cupped hands. Its scales shimmered like sapphires, its eyes pleading. "O King, save me from the bigger fish," it squeaked. I see that moment—Manu, his heart softening, gazing at the fish, its frailty stirring his compassion. He placed it in his water pot, promising safety. But by evening, the fish outgrew the pot, its fins brushing the rim. Astonished, Manu transferred it to a jar, then a pond, then a lake, and finally the ocean, as the fish grew larger each day. I feel his wonder—a king marveling at a miracle, sensing divinity in the creature's eyes.

In the ocean, the fish revealed its true form—a colossal golden fish with a horn, its body vast as a mountain, its voice deep as thunder. "I am Matsya, Vishnu's incarnation," it said. "A great flood will soon drown the earth. Build a boat, O Manu, and gather the seven sages, seeds of every plant, and pairs of every creature.

I will guide you." I see Manu's awe—his knees trembling, his heart racing, yet his faith unwavering. He bowed, "O Lord, I obey." Matsya vanished into the waves, leaving Manu with a divine mission. I feel his burden—a king tasked with saving life itself, his heart heavy yet resolute.

Manu returned to his kingdom; his mind ablaze with purpose. He summoned the seven sages—Vashishta, Kashyapa, Atri, Vishwamitra, Gautama, Bharadwaja, and Jamadagni—whose wisdom was the world's anchor. I see them—white-bearded, their eyes glowing with tapasya, their presence calming Manu's fears. He shared Matsya's warning, and they chanted mantras, blessing his task. Manu ordered a massive boat built, its wood carved with prayers, its hull strong as faith. I envision the scene—carpenters hammering, villagers weaving ropes, Manu overseeing with quiet strength, his heart whispering Vishnu's name.

As the boat rose, Manu roamed the earth, gathering seeds—rice, wheat, mango, neem—each a promise of tomorrow. He called animals—elephants trumpeting, deer bounding, snakes slithering, birds soaring—each pair a thread in life's tapestry. I see him—Manu, his robes dusty, his hands gentle, coaxing a frightened fawn, his voice soothing a tiger. The sages guided him, their prayers shielding the creatures from fear. I feel his love—a king who saw every life as sacred, his heart a vessel for Vishnu's will.

The skies darkened, clouds swelling like mountains. Rivers roared, seas surged, and the earth trembled. The flood began, its waters swallowing villages, forests, and mountains. I hear the chaos—people screaming, trees snapping, the world dissolving into a watery abyss. Manu, the sages, and the creatures boarded the boat, their faces etched with trust. Matsya appeared, his horn gleaming, and Manu tied the boat to it with Vasuki, the serpent king, as a rope. I see that divine voyage—Matsya swimming through the deluge, the boat bobbing, Manu praying, the sages chanting, animals huddling, a fragile ark in an endless sea.

The flood raged for years, the earth submerged, its sins washed away. Matsya guided the boat through towering waves, his voice calming Manu's doubts. "Fear not, O King, I am with you," he said. I feel Manu's faith—his heart clinging to Matsya's words, his eyes fixed on the horizon. The sages narrated Vishnu's glories, their stories keeping hope alive. I hear their voices—tales of creation, of dharma's triumph, weaving a thread of courage through the darkness.

One day, the waters receded, revealing the Himalayas' peaks. Matsya guided the boat to a summit, later called Manusyalaya, "Manu's abode." I see that landing—the boat resting, the sages stepping onto earth, animals leaping free, Manu's tears of gratitude falling. Matsya instructed, "O Manu, sow the seeds, nurture life, and teach dharma. You are the father of a new age." Manu bowed, his heart full. Matsya smiled, his form dissolving into the dawn, leaving a golden glow. I feel that renewal—a world reborn, Manu's mission complete, Vishnu's grace eternal.

Manu and the sages rebuilt civilization, planting seeds, guiding animals, and teaching dharma. Manu's descendants became the human race, his legacy a world rooted in righteousness. I see his kingdom—fields blooming, rivers singing, people praying, dharma's light restored. The Matsya Purana, sung by sages, immortalized his tale, revered during Matsya Jayanti. I feel his spirit—Manu, a king whose faith saved life, his story a beacon of hope.

This story is of faith, divine protection, and renewal. It teaches that God's compassion guides us through the darkest floods, and faith can rebuild a world. Matsya's grace and Manu's devotion live in my heart, like a river that never dries, promising life's eternal return.

And so, the story of Matsya Avatar and the Great Flood flows with divine mercy, human faith, and life's renewal. Drawn from the Matsya Purana, it echoes in temples and hearts, especially during Matsya Jayanti, reminding us that God protects the faithful. It teaches that faith can weather any storm, and dharma restores what's lost. Matsya's guidance and Manu's courage inspire us, showing that divine love is a lifeline in chaos. Whenever I see a fish in a river, I feel Matsya's presence, whispering of salvation and hope.

Story 18: Amba and Bhishma's Vow

The tale of Amba and Bhishma's Vow is a river of sorrow and fire, weaving a saga of vengeance, honor, and dharma's tangled paths, where every tear tells a story of sacrifice and struggle. Found in the Mahabharata, it's the story of Amba, a princess wronged by fate, and Bhishma, a warrior bound by an unyielding vow, their destinies colliding in a storm of human and divine. Amba, her spirit burning for justice, and Bhishma, his honor a fortress of dharma, are the heart of this epic. This story pierces my soul, teaching that human choices, even noble ones, birth pain, and dharma's complexities demand courage, sacrifice, and surrender. Let's journey to a time when a woman's quest for justice challenged an immortal vow, and her pain reshaped destiny.

In the golden age of Hastinapura, where the Ganges flowed like a silver thread of time, ruled King Shantanu, whose son, Devavrata, was known as Bhishma, the one of the terrible oaths. Bhishma, born to Ganga, was a warrior without equal, his heart a shrine to dharma. To secure his father's happiness, he swore a vow of lifelong celibacy and renounced the throne, a sacrifice that shook the heavens. I see Bhishma—tall, his silver hair flowing like a river, his eyes deep as ancient wisdom, a pillar of righteousness, yet bound by duty's iron chains. His vow was

Hastinapura's pride, a beacon of honor, but also a shadow that would darken lives. I feel his solitude—a man who traded love for duty, his heart a silent offering to his father's joy.

Far from Hastinapura, in the kingdom of Kashi, lived three princesses—Amba, Ambika, and Ambalika—daughters of the king, their beauty sung by bards across Bharat. Amba, the eldest, was a flame of grace and will, her eyes fierce with dreams, her heart woven with love for King Salva, a young ruler who had won her in secret promises. I see Amba—her raven hair cascading, her laughter like temple bells, her spirit yearning for a life of love, yet bound by her father's duty to forge alliances. A grand swayamvara was announced for the sisters, where princes would vie for their hands. I feel her hope—a princess on the cusp of joy, her heart dancing with visions of Salva's smile, unaware of the storm awaiting her.

Bhishma, tasked with securing brides for his half-brother

Vichitravirya, Hastinapura's heir, rode to Kashi, his mission to strengthen the Kuru dynasty. Uninvited, he entered the swayamvara arena, his presence a thunderclap. With Kshatriya custom, he challenged all suitors, declaring the princesses Vichitravirya's brides. I see that chaos—Amba's scream piercing the air, Ambika and Ambalika clinging to each other, Kashi's warriors falling like leaves under Bhishma's arrows, his face stern, duty his only guide. The princesses were swept onto his chariot, their dreams shattered, their voices drowned in the clatter of hooves. I feel Amba's terror—her world upended, her love for Salva torn away, a woman reduced to a prize of war.

In Hastinapura's grand palace, Amba found her voice amidst her sorrow. Standing before Bhishma, her eyes blazing, she said, "O Bhishma, I am pledged to Salva, my heart his. I cannot marry Vichitravirya." I see her courage—a princess, trembling yet defiant, her truth a sword against a titan. Bhishma, his heart stirred by her honesty, respected her plea. "Go to Salva with honor," he said, sending her with an escort. I feel his fairness—a warrior bound by dharma, yet unaware that his act of justice would birth a tragedy.

Amba reached Salva's kingdom, her heart fluttering with hope. But Salva, his pride wounded, turned cold. "You were claimed by Bhishma's might," he said, his voice sharp. "I cannot accept another's prize." I see Amba's heartbreak—her love rejected, her honor stained through no fault of her own, her dreams crumbling like ash. She pleaded, her tears falling, but Salva turned away, his court silent. I feel her despair—a woman abandoned, her identity stripped, standing alone in a world that judged her.

Amba returned to Hastinapura, her sorrow now a furnace of rage. She confronted Bhishma in the royal court, her voice a storm. "You caused my ruin, Bhishma. Marry me, or face my curse." Bhishma, his face heavy with regret, replied, "My vow of celibacy is unbreakable, Amba. I cannot." I see that clash—Amba's burning need for justice, Bhishma's vow an unyielding wall, two dharmas locked in a tragic duel. The court watched, breathless, as Amba's tears fell, her dignity shattered. I feel her pain—a woman betrayed by honor, her life a casualty of another's oath.

Amba left Hastinapura, her heart a vow of vengeance. She wandered forests and kingdoms, her royal silks now rags, her eyes fierce with purpose. She sought allies, but kings trembled at Bhishma's name, refusing to aid her. I see her—a lone figure, her feet blistered, her voice hoarse, pleading with warriors, her quest consuming her soul. She turned to penance, retreating to a Himalayan cave, her body wasting under the sun and snow, her prayers to Lord Shiva a cry of anguish. I feel her resolve—her pain forged into a weapon, her heart a battlefield of grief and fire.

Shiva, moved by her tapasya, appeared, his trident gleaming, his eyes soft with compassion. "Amba, your pain has reached me," he said. "In your next birth, you will slay Bhishma. Take this garland—only your destined form can wear it." I see that divine moment—Amba, trembling, clutching the garland, her heart alight with purpose. She hung it on a sacred tree, vowing to return, and entered a pyre, her body consumed, her soul soaring to rebirth. I feel her sacrifice—her life surrendered for justice; her spirit unbowed.

Amba was reborn as Shikhandi, daughter to King Drupada of Panchala, but raised as a son, her true identity a secret. I see Shikhandi—Amba's fire in her eyes, her heart heavy with a past life's wound, training with bow and sword, her destiny a shadow she sensed but could not name. Years later, on the Kurukshetra battlefield, Shikhandi faced Bhishma, the garland now hers. Bhishma, recognizing Amba's soul, lowered his weapons, honoring his vow not to fight a woman's essence. Arjuna, guided by Krishna, struck Bhishma through Shikhandi's presence, fulfilling Amba's quest. I see Bhishma's fall—his body a bed of arrows, his eyes calm, accepting dharma's decree. I feel Amba's triumph—her pain avenged, Shiva's justice complete, yet tinged with sorrow for Bhishma's nobility.

Shikhandi's role faded, but Amba's story endured, a testament to dharma's intricate dance. I hear her legacy—sung in tales of courage, reminding us that justice, even when righteous, carries a cost. This story is of vengeance, honor, and dharma's complexity. It teaches that pain can fuel justice, but dharma seeks balance beyond human strife. Amba's fire and Bhishma's vow stir my heart, like a river finding peace after a storm.

And so, the tale of Amba and Bhishma's Vow, drawn from the Mahabharata, weaves a tapestry of vengeance, sacrifice, and dharma's grace. It echoes in teachings and hearts, reminding us that dharma endures through pain. It teaches that a woman's courage can reshape fate, and dharma's path is both human and divine. Amba's quest and Bhishma's honor inspire us, showing that even in conflict, dharma seeks harmony. When I see Bhishma's bed of arrows, I feel Amba's spirit finding peace, her justice eternal.

Story 19: Varaha Avatar and the Rescue of Bhudevi

The story of Varaha Avatar and the Rescue of Bhudevi touches my heart like a sacred shrine, where waves of divine love and the earth's cry resound. Found in the Varaha Purana, this is the tale of Lord Vishnu's third incarnation as Varaha—a colossal boar—and the liberation of the earth from a demon's clutches. Bhudevi, our Mother Earth, and Varaha, whose love and power rose to protect her, are the soul of this saga. This story fills me with awe and devotion, teaching that God's love can pierce any darkness, and His strength delivers us from every crisis. Let's journey to a time when the earth sank into the abyss, a divine boar lifted her on his tusks, and love gave creation new life.

In the early dawn of creation, when the world was newborn, the earth was a lush mother, her womb nurturing rivers, forests, and life. She was Bhudevi, a form of Lakshmi, cradling Brahma's creation. I see her—Bhudevi, her form like green silk, her eyes brimming with compassion, her heart beating for every creature. But as ages turned, sin and pride darkened the hearts of humans and demons. Dharma weakened, and the earth's burden grew heavy. I feel that sorrow—Bhudevi's breaths labored, her rivers wilting, like a mother weeping for her children's pain.

In this era, Hiranyaksha, a mighty demon, was born. He was the brother of Hiranyakashipu, whose pride we've heard of before. Hiranyaksha's heart was filled with cruelty and greed. I see him—towering, his eyes burning like coals, his laughter a roar, as if he were darkness itself. He performed severe penance for Brahma, standing on one leg for years, his body covered in ants, yet his resolve unshaken. Brahma appeared, and Hiranyaksha asked for a boon: "Let no creature kill me, not by day or night, not in water or on land." Brahma granted the boon, and Hiranyaksha's arrogance soared to the heavens. I sense the danger of that moment—a demon, nearly immortal, ready to crush creation underfoot.

Hiranyaksha unleashed havoc on earth. He plundered kingdoms, burned sages' ashrams, and churned the oceans into chaos. His pride grew so vast that he dragged the earth itself into the cosmic ocean's abyss, known as Rasatala. I see that tragedy—Bhudevi, bound by the demon's hands, sinking into the ocean's depths, her cries echoing to the heavens. The earth's balance faltered—rivers dried, mountains trembled, and creatures quaked in fear. Bhudevi called out to Vishnu, "O Lord, save me!" I feel her plea—a mother weeping for her children, her faith in Vishnu's grace unwavering.

Vishnu, the preserver of creation, heard Bhudevi's cry. A storm of love and anger rose in His heart. I see Him—Vishnu, in Vaikuntha, His form like a blue cloud, His eyes gleaming with compassion and resolve. He took the form of Varaha—a massive boar, its body vast as a mountain, tusks shining like diamonds, its roar tearing the skies. I feel that divine form—Varaha, neither beast nor god, a force to challenge Hiranyaksha's boon. He plunged into the cosmic ocean, His body slicing through waves, His purpose to free Bhudevi. I see that journey—Varaha diving into the dark abyss, His heart beating for her.

In Rasatala, Hiranyaksha saw Varaha. His pride flared. "A boar? You dare challenge me?" he roared. A fierce battle began. I witness that war—Varaha charging with his tusks, clashing against Hiranyaksha, his roar shaking the ocean; Hiranyaksha striking with his mace, his cruelty a dark force. The ocean boiled, waves crashing to the heavens, as if creation itself bore witness. Varaha's fury was born of love, each blow for Bhudevi's freedom. I feel His devotion—a God fighting for His beloved Earth.

At last, Varaha seized Hiranyaksha on his tusks and hurled him into the sky—neither water nor land. With his tusks, He tore him apart, shattering Hiranyaksha's boon, his pride crumbling to dust. I see that victory—Hiranyaksha's blood flowing into the ocean, Varaha's roar proclaiming triumph. Varaha gently lifted Bhudevi on his tusks, like a lover cradling his beloved. I feel that love—Varaha raising her to the surface, His form glistening, Bhudevi's eyes filled with gratitude.

Varaha restored Bhudevi, mending her mountains, flowing her rivers, and reviving her life. Bhudevi bowed to Him, "O Lord, You gave me life." Varaha smiled, "I will always protect you." I see their reunion—Varaha and Bhudevi, bound by love and duty, like a mother and her guardian. His form faded into the dawn, but His grace lingered on earth. I feel His power—Varaha, worshipped in temples today, shielding devotees from peril.

This story is of love, duty, and liberation. It teaches that God's love can pierce any darkness, and faith can renew the earth. Varaha's roar and Bhudevi's cry kindle a fire in my heart, saying the Lord is ever our protector.

And so, the story of Varaha Avatar and the Rescue of Bhudevi, drawn from the Varaha Purana, resounds with divine love, sacrifice, and earth's salvation. It echoes in temples, especially during Varaha Jayanti, reminding us that God hears every cry. It teaches that love and faith rise above any abyss. Varaha's grace and Bhudevi's devotion inspire us, showing that divine love endures. When I see the earth's greenery, I hear Varaha's roar, promising eternal salvation.

Story 20: Shakuntala and Dushyanta

The tale of Shakuntala and Dushyanta is like a tender song to me, flowing with the rhythm of love, betrayal, and reunion, yet each note carries the depth of sorrow and hope. Found in the Mahabharata, this is a love story that begins in simplicity, passes through pain, and ends in faith. Shakuntala, an ashram's daughter whose heart overflowed with love, and Dushyanta, a king whose love endured time's test, are the soul of this saga. This story touches my heart, teaching that true love overcomes every obstacle, and faith can mend broken bonds. Let's journey to a time when a forest girl and a king's love became immortal, and sorrow deepened their bond.

Long ago, when dharma and truth reigned on earth, Hastinapura was ruled by the Chandravanshi kings. Dushyanta, a young and mighty king, was beloved by his people. I see him—Dushyanta, his face shining like the sun, his eyes bright with courage and gentleness, his heart a blend of warrior and lover. He loved hunting, and one day, with his soldiers, he ventured into a dense forest where Sage Kanva's ashram stood. I picture that forest—lush green trees, the scent of flowers, and birdsong, like a corner of paradise.

In Kanva's ashram lived Shakuntala, the daughter of Sage Vishwamitra and the apsara Menaka. Menaka had abandoned her at birth, and Kanva raised her as his own. Shakuntala grew up in nature's lap, her beauty as simple yet enchanting as the forest's blooms. I see her—Shakuntala, her eyes like a doe's, her smile like morning dew, her heart full of love and devotion. She tended flowers in the ashram, fed deer, and served Kanva, her life a melody of simplicity. I feel her purity—a daughter whose heart was as vast as the forest.

Dushyanta, wandering during his hunt, reached the ashram. Shakuntala welcomed him, offering water and fruits. I see that meeting—Dushyanta gazing at Shakuntala, his heart dancing to an unknown tune; Shakuntala, shy yet captivated, lost in his eyes. Love sprouted between them, like a seed kissed by rain. Dushyanta professed his love, and through the Gandharva rite of marriage, they vowed to be one. I feel that love—Dushyanta giving her a ring engraved with his name, Shakuntala's heart trembling with joy.

Dushyanta had to return to the capital, but he promised, "I'll return to make you my queen." Shakuntala trusted him, clutching his ring close to her heart. But time tests love harshly. Shakuntala, awaiting Dushyanta, was soon to become a mother. I see her loneliness—Shakuntala in the ashram, caressing her unborn child, her eyes wet with memories of Dushyanta. One day, Sage Durvasa visited the ashram. Lost in thoughts of Dushyanta, Shakuntala failed to serve him promptly. Furious,

Durvasa cursed her, “The one you dream of will forget you.” I feel the curse’s cruelty—Shakuntala, innocent, punished for her love, her heart breaking.

Shakuntala confessed to Kanva. He blessed her, “Daughter, give birth to your son. Truth will prevail.” She bore a son, named Sarvadaman, later Bharat, a boy as radiant as his parents. I see him—Shakuntala’s child, his laughter echoing in the forest, his strength taming lion cubs, her pride and pain. I feel her love—a mother whose heart held hope and sorrow for her son and his father.

Years passed, and Kanva sent Shakuntala to Hastinapura with her son. She stood in Dushyanta’s court, her beauty dimmed by hardship, her eyes fierce with truth. “O King, I am your wife,” she said, holding Sarvadaman’s hand. But Dushyanta, his memory veiled by the curse, denied her. “I know no such bond,” he said, his voice distant. I see Shakuntala’s heartbreak—her dignity shattered, her love questioned, a woman scorned before a court. She pleaded, her tears falling, but the curse held firm. I feel her despair—a mother and wife, rejected, her truth a flame in a storm.

As Shakuntala turned to leave, a divine voice boomed, “Dushyanta, she speaks truth. Accept your son.” The curse lifted, and Dushyanta’s memory returned. He saw Shakuntala, his heart breaking at her pain. “Forgive me,” he wept, embracing her and Sarvadaman. I see that reunion—Shakuntala, her tears of joy, her son beaming, the court celebrating dharma’s triumph. Dushyanta made her queen, and Bharat grew into a king whose name became India's.

This story is of love, trust, and reunion. It teaches that true love endures betrayal, and dharma heals broken bonds. I feel Shakuntala's faith—a melody that lives in temples and hearts, reminding us that love's truth prevails.

And so, the tale of Shakuntala and Dushyanta, drawn from the Mahabharata, sings a song of love, dharma, and reunion's grace. It echoes in teachings, teaching that faith endures through pain. It reminds me—love's truth triumphs. Shakuntala's love and Bharat's legacy inspire us, showing that dharma mends hearts. When I hear her tale, I feel her heartbeat, her love eternal.

Story 21: Narakasura's Defeat by Krishna

The story of Narakasura's Defeat by Krishna and Satyabhama washes over my heart like a sacred wave, carrying whispers of divine justice, love's power, and the triumph of light over darkness. Found in the Bhagavata Purana, this is the tale of Lord Krishna, the divine cowherd, and his beloved wife Satyabhama, who together vanquished the demon Narakasura, freeing the earth from his tyranny. Krishna, whose wisdom and charm guide the world, Satyabhama, whose courage blazes like fire, and the countless souls freed by their grace are the heart of this saga. This story fills me with awe, teaching that love and righteousness can conquer even the deepest evil, and divine partnership restores hope. Let's journey to a time when a demon's shadow darkened the earth, a divine couple rose to slay him, and light bloomed anew, celebrated as Deepavali.

In the age of Dwapara Yuga, when the earth was vibrant yet shadowed by evil, the city of Dwarka shone like a jewel by the sea. Here ruled Krishna, the eighth avatar of Vishnu, whose flute enchanted hearts and whose wisdom upheld dharma. I see him—Krishna, his skin dark as a monsoon cloud, his eyes twinkling with mischief and love, his smile a promise of salvation. Beside him was Satyabhama, one of his eight queens, a warrior princess whose beauty rivaled the dawn and whose spirit burned with courage. I see her—Satyabhama, her eyes fierce yet tender, her hands skilled with bow and sword, her heart fiercely devoted to Krishna. Their love was a divine dance, a partnership of equals, rooted in trust and dharma. I feel their bond—a love that strengthened them to face any storm.

Far from Dwarka, in the kingdom of Pragjyotishapura, ruled Narakasura, a demon born of Bhudevi and Varaha, yet corrupted by pride and power. I see him—Narakasura, his form towering, his eyes cold as stone, his laughter cruel, wielding weapons forged in dark rituals. Blessed with boons from Brahma, he believed himself invincible, his heart twisted by the demon Banasura's influence. Narakasura's tyranny spread like a plague—he plundered kingdoms, defiled sacred groves, and kidnapped 16,100 princesses, imprisoning them in his fortress. I hear their cries—women torn from their homes, their dignity shattered, their prayers rising to the heavens. He even stole the earrings of Aditi, the mother of the gods, and seized celestial treasures. I feel the earth's anguish—Bhudevi, Narakasura's own mother, weeping for her son's sins, her heart torn between love and justice.

The gods, led by Indra, pleaded with Krishna in Dwarka. "O Lord, Narakasura's evil threatens dharma. Only you can slay him," they said. Krishna's heart stirred with resolve, but his eyes turned to Satyabhama. "Will you ride with me, my love?" he asked. Satyabhama's face lit with purpose. "To the end, my Lord," she vowed. I see that moment—Krishna and Satyabhama, their hearts aligned, their love a shield against evil. Krishna summoned Garuda, his divine eagle, and with Satyabhama, soared toward Pragjyotishapura. I feel their determination—a divine couple, ready to restore light, their chariot a streak of hope across the sky.

Pragjyotishapura was a fortress of darkness, surrounded by mountains, rivers, and magical barriers crafted by Narakasura's ally, the demon Mura. I see it—walls of black stone, skies heavy with smoke, the air thick with fear. As Krishna's chariot approached, Mura and his five sons attacked, their weapons blazing. Krishna, with his Sudarshana Chakra, slew them effortlessly, earning the title "Murari," slayer of Mura. I witness that battle—Krishna, his chakra spinning like a sun, Satyabhama's arrows flying true, Garuda's wings scattering enemies. The barriers fell, and the fortress lay open, a challenge to Narakasura's pride.

Narakasura emerged, his army vast as the ocean, riding elephants and wielding dark sorcery. I see him—his armor gleaming with stolen gems, his eyes burning with defiance, his voice mocking Krishna. "A cowherd dares face me?" he sneered. The battle erupted, shaking the earth. Krishna fought with divine grace, his mace and chakra felling demons, while Satyabhama's arrows pierced Narakasura's generals. I see her—Satyabhama, her bow taut, her face fierce, fighting not just for victory but for the women imprisoned, her heart blazing with justice. I feel their unity—Krishna and Satyabhama, a divine team, their love amplifying their strength.

Narakasura, wounded yet defiant, turned his sorcery on Krishna, casting illusions of fire and serpents. Krishna smiled, dispelling them with a glance, his flute's silent melody calming the chaos. Satyabhama, seeing Narakasura's cruelty, urged Krishna, "End his tyranny, my Lord." Krishna nodded, but in a divine leela, he allowed Satyabhama to strike the final blow, honoring her as Bhudevi's incarnation. I see that moment—Satyabhama, her arrow glowing with divine fire, piercing Narakasura's heart, his body falling, his pride shattered. Narakasura, in his final breath, saw Krishna's divinity and found redemption, his soul freed from evil.

Krishna and Satyabhama entered the fortress, freeing the 16,100 princesses. I see them—women, their faces etched with pain yet lit with hope, bowing to their saviors, their tears of gratitude falling like rain. Krishna returned Aditi's earrings, restoring celestial honor. Bhudevi appeared, her eyes heavy with sorrow and relief. "My son's sins are cleansed by your grace," she said. Krishna smiled, "Dharma prevails, Mother." I feel that restoration—light returning to Pragjyotishapura, the earth breathing freely, love and justice triumphant.

Krishna married the princesses to honor them, giving them a life of dignity in Dwarka. The day of Narakasura's defeat became Deepavali, the festival of lights, celebrating light's victory over darkness. I see those lamps—flickering in every home, echoing

Krishna and Satyabhama's triumph, their love a beacon of hope. This story is of justice, love, and divine partnership. It teaches that righteousness, fueled by love, conquers evil, and faith lights even the darkest night. Krishna's smile and Satyabhama's courage live in my heart, like a lamp that never fades.

And so, the story of Narakasura's Defeat by Krishna and Satyabhama, drawn from the Bhagavata Purana, glows with divine justice, love's triumph, and light's return. It echoes in temples and homes during Deepavali, reminding us that dharma prevails. It teaches that love and faith can slay any demon. Krishna's grace and Satyabhama's valor inspire us, showing that divine partnership restores hope. When I light a Deepavali lamp, I feel their presence, whispering of victory and love eternal.

Story 22: Harishchandra's Truth

The tale of Harishchandra's Truth pierces my soul like a sacred vow, weaving a saga of unwavering honesty, sacrifice, and divine grace that leaves the heart trembling with awe. Found in the Markandeya Purana, this is the story of King Harishchandra, whose commitment to truth tested the limits of human endurance, and whose faith won the gods' blessings. Harishchandra, a king whose word was his life, his wife Taramati, whose love sustained him, and their son Rohitashva, a child caught in their trials, are the heart of this epic. This story fills me with reverence, teaching that truth, though painful, leads to salvation, and divine grace rewards the steadfast. Let's journey to a time when a king's vow shook the heavens, his sacrifices broke hearts, and truth shone brighter than the sun.

In the golden age of the Suryavanshi dynasty, the kingdom of Ayodhya flourished under King Harishchandra, a ruler famed for his truthfulness. I see him—Harishchandra, tall and regal, his eyes deep with wisdom, his voice gentle yet firm, his heart a temple of dharma. His queen, Taramati, was his equal in virtue, her beauty soft as moonlight, her love for him unyielding. I see her—Taramati, her smile a balm, her hands nurturing their son Rohitashva, a boy of seven whose laughter lit their palace. Ayodhya was a land of peace, where no one lied, no one starved, and Harishchandra's truth was its foundation. I feel his pride—a king whose word was law, his life a mirror of righteousness.

One day, Sage Vishwamitra, known for his fiery temper and divine wisdom, visited Ayodhya. I see him—Vishwamitra, his beard white, his eyes blazing with tapasya, his presence commanding respect. He sought to test Harishchandra's legendary truth, a trial born of divine curiosity. In a dream, Vishwamitra appeared to Harishchandra, demanding his kingdom as dakshina for a yagna. Harishchandra, bound by dharma, agreed without hesitation, signing away Ayodhya. I see that moment—Harishchandra, his hand steady, his heart heavy, yet his truth unshaken, believing his vow sacred.

Awakening, Harishchandra found Vishwamitra in his court, demanding the kingdom in reality. "Your dream was my will," the sage said. Harishchandra, true to his word, surrendered Ayodhya, his crown, and his wealth, leaving with Taramati and Rohitashva, clad in simple cloth. I see their departure—Ayodhya's people weeping, Taramati clutching Rohitashva, Harishchandra's face calm, his truth his only possession. I feel their pain—a royal family cast into poverty, their love their only shelter.

Vishwamitra's test deepened. He demanded a final dakshina of gold, knowing Harishchandra had none. The king, refusing to break his vow, sold himself, Taramati, and Rohitashva into slavery in Kashi to pay the sage. I see that heartbreak—Harishchandra, his voice breaking as he sold his family, Taramati's tears falling silently, Rohitashva clinging to her, unaware of their fate. Harishchandra became a servant at a cremation ground, Taramati a maid in a Brahmin's home, and Rohitashva a helper, their royal past a distant dream. I feel their despair—a king burning corpses, a queen scrubbing floors, their love strained yet unbroken.

Harishchandra's life at the cremation ground was grueling. I see him—his body smeared with ash, his hands blistered, collecting fees from mourners, his heart aching for his family. He never lied, even when tempted, his truth a flame in the darkness. Taramati, in her master's home, faced cruelty, her beauty faded, her thoughts only of Harishchandra and Rohitashva. I see her—her hands raw, her eyes searching for her son, her love her only strength. Rohitashva, separated, wandered Kashi's streets, his innocence dimming. I feel their separation—a family torn, their truth their only bond.

Tragedy struck when Rohitashva, chasing a deer, was bitten by a snake and died. Taramati, finding his body, wailed, her heart shattered. She carried him to the cremation ground, unaware Harishchandra worked there. I see that moment—Taramati, her son in her arms, her sobs echoing, Harishchandra recognizing them, his soul breaking yet his duty firm. "Pay the fee, or I cannot burn him," he said, bound by his master's rules, his voice trembling. Taramati, penniless, offered her tattered cloth, her dignity her final offering. I feel their agony—a husband and wife, united in loss, their truth tested to its core.

As Harishchandra prepared to burn his son, the heavens stirred. Vishwamitra appeared, his eyes soft with compassion, joined by Indra and Dharma. "Your truth has won, O King," they said. Rohitashva awoke, alive, his laughter ringing. I see that miracle—Harishchandra and Taramati embracing their son, their tears of joy falling, the gods blessing them. Vishwamitra restored Ayodhya, crowning Harishchandra once more, his kingdom radiant with truth. I feel that triumph—truth prevailing, divine grace rewarding sacrifice, love enduring.

Harishchandra ruled Ayodhya with even greater wisdom, his story sung by sages, revered in temples. I see his legacy—people vowing truth in his name, his tale a beacon of dharma. This story is of honesty, sacrifice, and divine grace. It teaches that truth, though painful, leads to salvation, and faith brings miracles. Harishchandra's vow and Taramati's love stir my heart, like a star guiding through the darkest night.

And so, the tale of Harishchandra's Truth, drawn from the Markandeya Purana, shines with unwavering honesty, sacrifice, and divine grace. It echoes in teachings and hearts, reminding us that truth endures. It teaches that sacrifice for dharma brings salvation. Harishchandra's vow and Taramati's devotion inspire us, showing that divine grace rewards the steadfast. When I think of Harishchandra, I feel his truth, a light eternal.

Story 23: Mohini and the Amrita Deception

The story of Mohini and the Amrita Deception touches my heart like a magical spell, where ripples of divine enchantment, cunning, and cosmic balance resound. Found in the Bhagavata Purana, this is the tale of Lord Vishnu's Mohini avatar, who used divine allure to protect the nectar of immortality from demons and grant it to the gods. Mohini, whose beauty captivated heaven and the netherworld, and Vishnu, whose wisdom preserved creation's balance, are the soul of this saga. This story fills me with awe and devotion, teaching that divine intelligence can overcome any evil, and righteousness always stands with truth. Let's journey to a time when the churning of the ocean birthed the nectar, a divine enchantress ensnared demon in illusion, and creation's harmony was preserved.

In an ancient age of creation, when gods and demons clashed for supremacy, a great crisis shook the heavens. The demons, led by mighty warriors, defeated the gods under Indra's command, seizing control of heaven. I see them—the gods, their strength faded, pleading before Vishnu in Vaikuntha, their eyes heavy with despair. Vishnu, the preserver of creation, heard their cries. I see Him—Vishnu, His form like a blue cloud, His eyes gleaming with compassion and cunning. He said, "Join the demons to churn the ocean of milk. The nectar of immortality will emerge, restoring your power." I feel His wisdom—Vishnu, knowing creation's balance, weaving a plan to save the gods.

Gods and demons united, using Mount Mandara as the churning rod and Vasuki, the serpent, as the rope to churn the Kshirasagara, the ocean of milk. I see that scene—the mountain sinking into the ocean, gods and demons pulling the rope, the sea frothing. Vishnu took the Kurma avatar, His tortoise form supporting the mountain. I feel His strength—Kurma, the foundation of creation, making the churning possible. From the ocean emerged Dhanvantari, Kamadhenu, and many treasures, but at last, the golden pot of Amrita, the nectar, appeared. I see it—a radiant vessel, glowing with nectar, the source of eternal life.

The demons lunged for the Amrita, their greed blazing in their eyes. I see their cruelty—demons like Ravana and Kamsa, ready to snatch the nectar, their arrogance eager to swallow creation. The gods, weaker than the demons, trembled in fear. Then Vishnu transformed into Mohini—a beauty so divine, her charm bewitched heaven and the netherworld. I see her—Mohini, her form like moonlight, her eyes woven with illusion, her smile a spell, as if creation itself adored her. Mohini took the pot of Amrita, and gods and demons alike bowed before her. I feel that enchantment—Mohini, binding hearts with a single glance.

In a voice sweet as honey, Mohini said, "I will distribute the nectar, but you must obey me." The demons, lost in her beauty, agreed. I see their folly—demons, invincible in might, ensnared by a beauty's spell. Mohini seated gods and demons in two rows and, with cunning, began serving the nectar to the gods first. I feel her cleverness—Mohini, saving dharma with every drop, her every smile distracting the demons.

But Rahu, a cunning demon, disguised himself as a god and slipped into the nectar line. I see him—Rahu, his eyes burning with greed, desperate to steal a sip of Amrita. As he drank, the Sun and Moon revealed his deception. Mohini swiftly hurled the Sudarshana Chakra, severing Rahu's head from his body. I see that moment—Rahu's head, immortal from the nectar, soaring into the sky, his body collapsing. Rahu and Ketu were born, destined to eclipse the Sun and Moon. I feel Vishnu's justice—Mohini, punishing deceit, upholding dharma.

The demons realized Mohini's trick and rose in fury, ready for war. But the gods, empowered by the nectar, defeated them, reclaiming heaven. I see that victory—Indra on his throne, the gods radiant with strength, shining with Mohini's grace. Mohini's form faded, but Vishnu's illusion lingered in creation. I feel His power—Vishnu, as Mohini, saving dharma, balancing the cosmos.

This story is of divine wisdom, illusion, and righteousness. It teaches that truth and cunning together defeat evil, and divine grace protects creation. Mohini's smile and Vishnu's wisdom spark a magic in my heart, proclaiming that dharma always triumphs.

And so, the story of Mohini and the Amrita Deception, drawn from the Bhagavata Purana, resounds with divine enchantment, cunning, and cosmic balance. It echoes in temples, especially during Vishnu worship, reminding us that the Lord's illusion overcomes evil. It teaches that righteousness and wisdom rise above any crisis. Mohini's grace and Vishnu's cunning inspire us, showing that divine love and justice are eternal. When I see the ocean's waves, I glimpse Mohini's illusion, promising dharma's victory.

Story 24: King Shibi's Compassion

The tale of King Shibi's Compassion pierces my heart like a sacred sacrifice, weaving a saga of selfless love, mercy, and divine justice that leaves the soul trembling with reverence. Found in the Mahabharata, this is the story of King Shibi, whose compassion shook the heavens and whose sacrifice won the gods' blessings. Shibi, a king whose heart beat for every creature, and his mercy, which tested creation's laws, are the soul of this epic. This story fills me with awe, teaching that compassion is the greatest strength, and divine grace rewards the selfless. Let's journey to a time when a king's mercy challenged the gods, his sacrifice broke hearts, and compassion shone brighter than the sun.

In ancient times, when dharma's light graced the earth, the kingdom of Ushinar thrived under King Shibi, whose mercy and justice were famed across the three worlds. I see him—Shibi, tall and radiant, his eyes brimming with kindness, his voice a haven of peace, his heart open to every being. His queen, Sudeshna, matched his virtue, her beauty soft as flowers, her love his strength. I see her—Sudeshna, her smile like sunrise, her hands serving the people. Ushinar was a paradise, where no one went hungry, no one feared, and Shibi's compassion was its foundation. I feel his pride—a king whose kingdom was a temple of mercy.

One day, in heaven, Indra and Agni discussed Shibi's compassion. I see them—Indra, on his throne, his eyes sparkling with curiosity, Agni, his flames flickering with thought. Indra said, "Is Shibi's mercy boundless? Let us test him." Agni agreed, and they descended to earth. Indra took the form of a hawk, and Agni became a dove, fleeing from the hawk into Shibi's court. I see that scene—the dove, trembling with fear, seeking refuge in Shibi's lap, the hawk pursuing, its eyes sharp as a predator's.

The dove, in a quivering voice, pleaded, "O King, save me, I seek your protection." Shibi's heart melted. I feel his compassion—Shibi, shielding the dove in his arms, vowing to protect it. The hawk screeched, "This is my food; do not starve me." Shibi, calmly, said, "I will give you food, but this creature will not be harmed." The hawk challenged, "Give me flesh equal to its weight." Shibi ordered a scale, placing the dove on one side and cutting flesh from his own body to place on the other. I see that sacrifice—Shibi, slicing his flesh with a sword, his face free of pain, his eyes glowing with mercy.

But the scale didn't balance. Shibi cut more flesh, his blood flowing, yet the dove's side remained heavier. I feel his pain—Shibi, offering his body, Sudeshna weeping, the court stunned. Finally, Shibi climbed onto the scale himself, ready to give his life. I see that selflessness—Shibi, sacrificing everything for the dove, his heart an ocean of compassion. Then, the hawk and dove vanished, and Indra and Agni appeared, their faces shining with admiration.

"Your compassion has conquered us," Indra said. "Your name will live forever." I see that triumph—Shibi, his body healed, Sudeshna in his arms, the people cheering. Indra blessed him, and Shibi ruled with even greater mercy. I see his legacy—Shibi's tale, sung in temples, a symbol of compassion. This story is of mercy, sacrifice, and divine justice. It teaches that compassion is the greatest power, and divine grace rewards the selfless. Shibi's mercy lights a lamp in my heart, proclaiming that love wins every test.

And so, the tale of King Shibi's Compassion, drawn from the Mahabharata, shines with selfless mercy, sacrifice, and divine justice. It echoes in teachings and hearts, reminding us that compassion is eternal. It teaches that selfless sacrifice brings salvation. Shibi's mercy and sacrifice inspire us, showing that divine grace rewards the true-hearted. When I think of Shibi, I feel his compassion, a light eternal.

Story 25: Gajendra Moksha (The Liberation of Gajendra)

The story of Gajendra Moksha washes over my heart like a sacred river, carrying whispers of divine compassion, surrender, and salvation that touch the soul with profound faith. Found in the Bhagavata Purana, this is the tale of Gajendra, an elephant king, whose desperate cry to Lord Vishnu brought divine rescue, granting him liberation from the cycle of birth and death. Gajendra, whose strength bowed to humility, and Vishnu, whose love answers every sincere prayer, are the heart of this saga. This story fills me with awe, teaching that God hears the humblest call, and true surrender brings eternal freedom. Let's journey to a time when an elephant's struggle shook the heavens, a lotus-offering prayer reached Vaikuntha, and divine grace shone brighter than the sun.

In a golden age when the earth was lush and vibrant, a majestic forest bloomed near the Trikuta Mountain, cradled by rivers and alive with creatures. Here roamed Gajendra, the king of elephants, a mighty creature whose strength was unmatched, his heart gentle yet proud. I see him—Gajendra, his massive form like a moving hill, his trunk swaying, his eyes wise, leading his herd with care. His tusks gleamed like crescent moons, and his trumpets echoed through the trees, a sound that brought peace to the forest. Gajendra's herd—mothers, calves, and elders—followed him, their trust in him absolute. I feel his pride—a king whose love for his family was as vast as the forest itself.

The forest was a paradise, with sparkling lakes, blooming lotuses, and air sweet with flower scents. Gajendra's days were filled with joy—bathing in cool waters, playing with his calves, and resting under ancient banyan trees. I see those moments—Gajendra, spraying water on his herd, his deep rumbles like laughter, the calves tumbling in delight. But Gajendra's heart carried a faint memory, a whisper from a past life. Long ago, he was King Indradyumna, a devout Vishnu worshipper who ruled with righteousness. I see that king—Indradyumna, his eyes fixed on Vishnu's idol, his heart lost in prayer. But a curse by Sage Agastya, angered by the king's distraction during a visit, turned Indradyumna into an elephant, his human wisdom buried deep within Gajendra's soul.

One scorching day, Gajendra led his herd to a serene lake nestled in the forest, its surface covered with pink lotuses, its waters cool and inviting. I see that lake—its ripples catching the sun, bees humming over flowers, a haven of peace. Gajendra waded in, his herd following, their trunks splashing water, their trumpets joyful. But as Gajendra stood deep in the lake, a sudden force gripped his leg—a crocodile, fierce and relentless, clamped its jaws around him. I see that struggle—Gajendra, his eyes wide with shock, thrashing against the crocodile, the water churning into foam. The crocodile, strong and unyielding, pulled Gajendra deeper, its eyes cold with determination.

Gajendra fought with all his might, his tusks slashing, his trunk flailing, his roars shaking the forest. I feel his strength—Gajendra, a king refusing to yield, his herd trumpeting in panic on the shore. But the crocodile's grip was unbreakable, its power drawn from a curse. Long ago, the crocodile was Huhu, a gandharva who insulted Sage Devala and was cursed to live as a beast. The battle raged—days turned to months, months to years. I see Gajendra's anguish—his body weakening, his skin torn, his heart heavy with fear for his herd. The forest, once vibrant, grew silent, as if mourning its king's plight.

Gajendra's strength faded, his breaths labored, his herd helpless on the shore. I feel their despair—the elephants, their trunks drooping, their eyes wet, unable to save their leader. In his darkest moment, a spark of memory flickered in Gajendra's soul—the prayer of Indradyumna, the devotion to Vishnu. With his last strength, Gajendra plucked a lotus from the lake, raising it in his trunk as an offering. I see that moment—Gajendra, half-submerged, his body trembling, his trunk lifted to the sky, his heart crying, "O Narayana, Lord of the Universe, save me!" His voice, weak yet pure, pierced the heavens, a prayer of total surrender. I feel his faith—Gajendra, broken but unyielding, his soul reaching for divine grace.

In Vaikuntha, Vishnu heard Gajendra's cry, His heart stirred with love. I see Him—Vishnu, His form radiant as a thousand suns, His eyes soft with compassion, the Sudarshana Chakra spinning in His hand. He mounted Garuda, His divine eagle, and descended to the lake, the sky blazing with His presence. I see that descent—Garuda's wings thundering, Vishnu's conch echoing, the forest trembling with divine energy. Gajendra, nearly lifeless, saw Vishnu's form and felt a surge of hope. The crocodile tightened its grip, but Vishnu's chakra flashed, severing its jaws. I see that liberation—Gajendra, freed, stumbling to the shore, the crocodile's body still, its curse lifted.

Vishnu stepped toward Gajendra, His lotus feet touching the earth, His smile a balm. I see that reunion—Gajendra, his eyes brimming with tears, bowing his massive head, Vishnu's hand gently touching his trunk. "Your faith has saved you," Vishnu said. Gajendra's soul, purified by surrender, shed his elephant form, revealing Indradyumna, radiant and free. I feel that salvation—Indradyumna, his heart merged with Vishnu, granted moksha, liberated from rebirth. Huhu, the gandharva, also regained his celestial form, bowing to Vishnu's mercy. The herd trumpeted in joy, the forest blooming anew, as if celebrating divine grace.

Vishnu vanished, but His presence lingered in the lake, now a sacred site. I see that legacy—pilgrims visiting, offering lotuses, chanting Gajendra's prayer. This story is of faith, surrender, and divine compassion. It teaches that God hears every sincere cry, and true devotion brings eternal freedom. Gajendra's lotus and Vishnu's grace kindle a fire in my heart, proclaiming that divine love never fails.

And so, the story of Gajendra Moksha, drawn from the Bhagavata Purana, shines with divine compassion, surrender, and salvation's glory. It echoes in temples during Vishnu worship, reminding us that God answers every heartfelt prayer. It teaches that faith overcomes any crisis. Gajendra's surrender and Vishnu's grace inspire us, showing that divine love is eternal. When I see a lotus bloom, I hear Gajendra's prayer, promising salvation's hope.

Story 26: Yayati and Devayani

The tale of Yayati and Devayani grips my soul like a bittersweet song, weaving a saga of love, desire, betrayal, and wisdom that leaves the heart aching with lessons learned. Found in the Mahabharata, this is the story of King Yayati, whose pursuit of youth and pleasure led to joy and sorrow, and Devayani, whose love and pride shaped a dynasty's fate. Yayati, a king torn between passion and duty, Devayani, a woman of fiery love and vengeance, and their tangled bonds are the heart of this epic. This story fills me with wonder, teaching that desires are fleeting, but wisdom endures, and true love demands sacrifice. Let's journey to a time when a king's heart wandered, a woman's love tested fate, and a curse revealed life's deepest truths.

In the ancient Lunar dynasty, when the earth was ruled by noble kings, Yayati, son of Nahusha, reigned over a vast kingdom. I see him—Yayati, tall and charismatic, his eyes bright with ambition, his heart a mix of valor and desire, his charm winning hearts. Yayati was a warrior, his sword unmatched, yet his soul craved life's pleasures—music, beauty, and love. His kingdom flourished, its fields golden, its people content, but Yayati's heart was restless, seeking joys beyond the throne. I feel his yearning—a king who ruled the earth but sought to conquer time itself.

One day, while hunting in a dense forest, Yayati heard a woman's cry near a well. I see that scene—the forest, thick with vines, the well's dark mouth echoing with desperation. Curious, Yayati peered in and saw Devayani, a young woman, clinging to the well's edge, her face pale with fear. Devayani was the daughter of Shukracharya, the guru of the asuras, her beauty like a flame, her eyes fierce yet vulnerable. I see her—Devayani, her hair tangled, her voice trembling, yet her spirit unbroken. She had fallen into the well during a quarrel with Sharmishtha, the daughter of the asura king Vrishaparva, who pushed her in a fit of anger.

Yayati, moved by her plight, extended his hand, pulling Devayani to safety. I feel that moment—Devayani, grasping his hand, her heart racing, Yayati's strength her lifeline. As she stood before him, her wet clothes clinging, her eyes met his, sparking a silent bond. Devayani, proud and grateful, declared, "You've touched me, O king; by custom, you must marry me." Yayati, struck by her beauty and spirit, agreed, his heart stirred by love. I see their connection—Yayati,

captivated, Devayani, her pride softened by his kindness.

But Devayani's heart burned with anger toward Sharmishtha, her rival. I feel her wrath—Devayani, humiliated, vowing revenge. She returned to her father, Shukracharya, and recounted the insult. Shukracharya, whose power could revive the dead, confronted Vrishaparva, demanding justice. To appease him, Vrishaparva sent Sharmishtha to serve Devayani as a maid. I see

Sharmishtha—her beauty regal, her eyes defiant yet resigned, bowing to Devayani, her heart heavy with shame. Devayani, triumphant, agreed to marry Yayati, but insisted Sharmishtha accompany her as a servant to Yayati's palace. Yayati, unaware of the brewing storm, welcomed Devayani as his queen, their love blossoming like spring.

Yet Yayati's heart, ever restless, wandered to Sharmishtha, whose quiet grace and hidden sorrow drew him. I see their stolen glances—Sharmishtha, serving in the palace, her eyes meeting Yayati's, a forbidden spark igniting. In secret, they fell in love, their hearts defying Devayani's command. Yayati married Sharmishtha privately, and she bore him sons, including Puru. I feel their passion—Yayati, torn between duty and desire, Sharmishtha, her love a quiet rebellion. When Devayani learned of the betrayal, her heart shattered, her pride wounded. I see her fury—Devayani, confronting Yayati, her tears burning, her voice cursing him.

Devayani appealed to Shukracharya, who, in anger, cursed Yayati with old age, his youth stripped instantly. I see that curse—Yayati, his body wrinkled, his strength gone, his heart breaking at life's joys lost. He pleaded, "Spare me, for my heart still craves youth." Shukracharya relented, allowing Yayati to exchange his old age with a son's youth. Yayati asked his sons, but only Puru, Sharmishtha's son, agreed, giving his youth to his father. I feel Puru's sacrifice—Puru, young and noble, aging for his father's happiness.

Yayati, youthful again, indulged in pleasures, his heart chasing endless joys. I see him—Yayati, surrounded by beauty, music, and love, yet his soul growing hollow. Years passed, and Yayati realized desires were fleeting, leaving only emptiness. I feel his awakening—Yayati, weary of pleasure, seeking wisdom. He returned his youth to Puru, embracing old age, and retired to the forest, his heart seeking peace. Yayati blessed Puru, naming him his heir, whose lineage led to the Pandavas and Kauravas. I see his legacy—Yayati, a king who learned life's truth, his story sung in courts.

This story is of love, desire, betrayal, and wisdom. It teaches that pleasures fade, but wisdom endures, and sacrifice builds legacies. Yayati's journey and Devayani's love stir my heart, like a song of life's fleeting joys and eternal truths.

And so, the tale of Yayati and Devayani, drawn from the Mahabharata, sings of love, desire, betrayal, and wisdom's triumph. It echoes in teachings, reminding us that wisdom outlives pleasure. It teaches that sacrifice shapes destinies. Yayati's journey and Devayani's passion inspire us, showing that life's lessons lead to peace. When I hear Yayati's tale, I feel his heart, seeking eternal truth.

Story 27: Arjuna's Quest for Divine Weapons

The story of Arjuna's Quest for Divine Weapons sets my heart ablaze like a warrior's resolve, weaving a saga of courage, discipline, and divine favor that echoes with the clash of celestial arms. Found in the Mahabharata, this is the tale of Arjuna, the Pandava archer, whose journey to the heavens to secure divine weapons ensured dharma's triumph in the Kurukshetra war. Arjuna, whose skill and devotion won the gods' blessings, and the divine beings who tested and rewarded him, are the heart of this epic. This story fills me with awe, teaching that dedication and humility earn divine grace, and true warriors fight for righteousness. Let's journey to a time when a hero's resolve shook the heavens, his penance won celestial favor, and divine weapons lit the path to justice.

In the age of the Dwapara Yuga, when the earth trembled under the weight of adharma, the Pandavas, five noble brothers, faced exile in the forests of Kamyaka, their hearts heavy with injustice. I see them—the Pandavas, Yudhishthira's wisdom, Bhima's strength, Arjuna's grace, and the twins' loyalty, their bond unbreakable despite their trials. Arjuna, the third Pandava, was a peerless archer, his bow Gandiva a legend, his eyes sharp with purpose. I see him—Arjuna, his form lithe and powerful, his heart burning with love for his brothers and a vow to restore their honor. The Pandavas had been cheated of their kingdom by their cousins, the Kauravas, in a rigged dice game, their wife Draupadi humiliated. I feel Arjuna's resolve—a warrior whose heart ached for justice; his mind set on preparing for the inevitable war.

One evening, as the Pandavas sat by a forest fire, Sage Vyasa, the seer of truth, visited them. I see him—Vyasa, his eyes deep with wisdom, his voice carrying destiny's weight. "The Kauravas grow stronger, their allies vast. Only divine weapons can ensure your victory," he said, turning to Arjuna. "Seek the gods' favor, O Partha, and gain the astras that will uphold dharma." Arjuna nodded, his heart stirred with purpose. I feel that moment—Arjuna, his brothers' hopes resting on him, his soul ready to face any trial. Krishna, Arjuna's friend and divine guide, blessed him, saying, "Your heart is pure; the gods will aid you." I see Krishna—His smile a beacon, His words fueling Arjuna's courage.

Arjuna set out alone, his bow slung across his shoulder, his mind fixed on penance. He journeyed to the Himalayas, where snow-capped peaks touched the sky, and sacred rivers sang of divinity. I see that landscape—mountains gleaming under starlight, air crisp with purity, forests whispering ancient secrets. Arjuna chose a secluded spot by the Ganga, its waters sparkling like diamonds. He began a fierce tapasya, standing on one leg, his arms raised, his eyes closed, chanting Shiva's name. I see him—Arjuna, his body lean from fasting, his face serene, his heart a flame of devotion. Days turned to months, his penance shaking the earth, his resolve unyielding.

The gods, watching from the heavens, were moved by Arjuna's devotion, but Lord Shiva, the destroyer, decided to test him. I see Shiva—His form radiant, His third eye glowing, His trident a symbol of cosmic power. Disguised as a hunter, with Parvati as his companion, Shiva descended to the forest. At that moment, a wild boar, sent by the demon Muka, charged at Arjuna, disrupting his meditation. I see that chaos—Arjuna, his eyes snapping open, his bow drawn in a flash, the boar roaring. Arjuna's arrow flew, piercing the boar, but another arrow, Shiva's, struck it simultaneously. I feel the tension—Arjuna, confused, facing the hunter, his pride as an archer challenged.

"Who dares claim my kill?" Arjuna demanded. The hunter, Shiva in disguise, laughed, "Your arrow? Mine struck first." A heated duel began, Arjuna's arrows blazing, Shiva parrying with ease. I see that battle—Arjuna, his skill unmatched, yet his arrows vanishing against the hunter's might. Exhausted, Arjuna realized his opponent's divinity and fell to his knees, offering a garland of flowers to Shiva's image. I feel his humility—Arjuna, his pride shed, his heart open. Shiva revealed His true form, His smile divine. "Your courage and devotion have won me, Partha," He said, granting Arjuna the Pashupatastra, a weapon of cosmic destruction. I see that blessing—Shiva, His hand on Arjuna's head, the astra's power flowing into him.

Arjuna's quest continued. Indra, his divine father, invited him to Amaravati, the celestial city. I see that splendor—palaces of gold, apsaras dancing, gandharvas singing. Indra embraced Arjuna, gifting him thunderbolt astras and training him in celestial warfare. I feel Arjuna's growth—a warrior honed by divine guidance. Other gods—Varuna, Agni, Kubera—bestowed their astras, each weapon a spark of cosmic power. I see Arjuna—his quiver glowing, his heart humble yet fierce, ready to wield divine might for dharma.

Arjuna faced trials too. The apsara Urvashi, enamored, sought his love, but Arjuna, devoted to his mission, refused, earning her curse of temporary emasculation, later a boon in disguise for his exile's final year. I feel his discipline—Arjuna, resisting temptation, his heart fixed on duty. Returning to earth, Arjuna rejoined his brothers, his divine weapons a promise of victory. I see their reunion—the Pandavas, their eyes shining with hope, Krishna smiling, knowing dharma's triumph was near.

This story is of courage, discipline, and divine favor. It teaches that devotion and humility earn celestial grace, and true warriors fight for justice. Arjuna's quest and Shiva's blessing ignite a spark in my heart, proclaiming that dharma prevails through dedication.

And so, the story of Arjuna's Quest for Divine Weapons, drawn from the Mahabharata, shines with courage, discipline, and divine favor's glory. It echoes in warrior tales, reminding us that dedication wins divine aid. It teaches that righteousness triumphs through effort. Arjuna’s resolve and the gods’ grace inspire us, showing that divine support is eternal for the just. When I see an archer’s bow, I feel Arjuna’s strength, promising dharma’s victory.

Story 28: Nachiketa and Yama

The tale of Nachiketa and Yama pierces my soul like a ray of eternal truth, weaving a saga of curiosity, courage, and spiritual wisdom that leaves the heart trembling with enlightenment. Found in the Katha Upanishad, this is the story of Nachiketa, a young boy whose quest for truth led him to face Yama, the god of death, and uncover the secrets of life and immortality. Nachiketa, whose innocent heart sought ultimate knowledge, and Yama, whose wisdom unveiled the soul's eternity, are the heart of this profound narrative. This story fills me with reverence, teaching that fearlessness and curiosity lead to divine truth, and the soul is immortal. Let's journey to a time when a boy's questions shook the heavens, a god's answers lit the path to wisdom, and truth shone brighter than death itself.

In an ancient age when wisdom was sought through sacrifice, a sage named Vajasravasa lived in a modest hermitage, his heart devoted to Vedic rituals. I see him—Vajasravasa, his beard gray, his eyes fixed on sacred fires, his life a quest for divine favor. He had a son, Nachiketa, a boy of ten, whose eyes sparkled with curiosity, his heart pure and fearless. I see Nachiketa—small yet bright, his questions endless, his soul yearning for truth beyond rituals. Vajasravasa, seeking heavenly merit, decided to perform a grand yagna, offering his wealth to the gods. I feel the hermitage's energy—fires blazing, mantras echoing, sages gathered.

But Vajasravasa's heart wavered, his generosity tinged with attachment. He gave away old cows, barren and weak, unfit for true sacrifice. I see those cows—their ribs showing, their steps faltering, a mockery of giving. Nachiketa, watching, felt unease, his young mind sensing the flaw. "Father, a true gift is given with love. These cows bring no merit," he thought. Boldly, he asked, "To whom will you give me, Father?" I feel his courage—Nachiketa, his voice steady, his heart probing truth. Vajasravasa, irritated, ignored him, but Nachiketa persisted, asking thrice. In anger, Vajasravasa snapped, "To Yama, the god of death, I give you!"

Silence fell, the sages stunned, Vajasravasa's heart sinking with regret. But Nachiketa, unafraid, accepted his fate. "If I am offered to Yama, I will go," he said, his eyes calm. I see that resolve—Nachiketa, a boy facing death, his soul burning with purpose. He journeyed to Yama's abode, a realm beyond life, where souls await judgment. I see that world—shadows swirling, air heavy with finality, yet Nachiketa's heart unshaken. Yama was absent, attending cosmic duties, so Nachiketa waited at his door, fasting for three days and nights. I feel his patience—Nachiketa, hungry yet steadfast, his curiosity stronger than fear.

Yama returned, his form towering, his eyes deep with the weight of death. I see him—Yama, his noose in hand, his presence commanding, yet his heart moved by Nachiketa's resolve. "You waited without food, O boy. I owe you three boons for my absence," Yama said. Nachiketa's first boon was for his father's peace, that Vajasravasa be free of anger and blessed with prosperity. I feel his love—Nachiketa, selfless, seeking his father's happiness. Yama granted it, smiling at the boy's heart.

For his second boon, Nachiketa asked to learn the fire sacrifice that leads to heavenly realms. I see his curiosity—Nachiketa, eager for knowledge, his eyes fixed on Yama. Yama taught him the ritual, naming it the Nachiketa Agni, a path to celestial joy. I feel that teaching—Yama, his voice resonant, Nachiketa absorbing every word. But Nachiketa's heart sought deeper truth. For his third boon, he asked, "What happens after death? Does the soul live, or vanish? Tell me the truth, O Yama." I see that question—Nachiketa, fearless, his voice piercing the veil of mortality.

Yama hesitated, his eyes searching Nachiketa's soul. "Ask for wealth, kingdoms, or eternal youth, but not this," he urged. I feel Yama's caution—a god guarding cosmic secrets. But Nachiketa persisted, "Wealth fades, youth dies. I seek only truth." Moved by his resolve, Yama revealed the eternal wisdom. I see that moment—Yama, his voice like thunder, Nachiketa listening, his heart open. "The soul is immortal, beyond birth and death," Yama said. "It is Atman, one with Brahman, the cosmic truth. The body dies, but the soul journeys, shaped by karma." I feel that revelation—Nachiketa, his soul illuminated, Yama's words a lamp in the darkness.

Yama taught the path to liberation—control the senses, meditate on the Atman, and realize the self's unity with the divine. "Like a chariot, the body is driven by the soul, guided by wisdom," he said. I see Nachiketa—his eyes shining, his heart merging with truth. Yama blessed him, granting him liberation, his soul freed from rebirth. Nachiketa returned to earth, his body light, his wisdom vast. I feel his transformation—a boy now a sage, sharing Yama's teachings. Vajasravasa embraced him, his heart healed, the hermitage radiant with truth.

This story is of curiosity, courage, and eternal wisdom. It teaches that fearlessness seeks truth, and the soul is immortal. Nachiketa's questions and Yama's answers light a fire in my heart, proclaiming that wisdom conquers death.

And so, the tale of Nachiketa and Yama, drawn from the Katha Upanishad, shines with curiosity, courage, and eternal truth's glory. It echoes in Upanishadic teachings, reminding us that wisdom transcends mortality. It teaches that truth liberates the soul. Nachiketa's quest and Yama's wisdom inspire us, showing that divine truth is eternal. When I ponder life's mysteries, I hear Nachiketa's voice, promising enlightenment's light.

Story 29: Ekalavya's Sacrifice

The story of Ekalavya's Sacrifice pierces my heart like an arrow of loyalty, weaving a saga of dedication, sacrifice, and the bittersweet cost of dharma that leaves the soul trembling with both sorrow and reverence. Found in the Mahabharata, this is the tale of Ekalavya, a young tribal boy whose unparalleled devotion to archery and his guru led him to a sacrifice so profound that it echoes as a lesson in honor and the complexities of righteousness. Ekalavya, whose skill rivaled the greatest warriors, and Dronacharya, the guru torn between duty and compassion, are the heart of this poignant narrative. This story fills me with a mix of awe and heartache, teaching that true dedication demands sacrifices that can break the heart, yet uphold dharma in ways that are both noble and tragic. Let's journey to a time when a boy's dream clashed with the harsh laws of society, his sacrifice became a legend, and his loyalty lit a bittersweet flame of justice.

In the age of the Dwapara Yuga, when the earth was a stage for great warriors and greater destinies, the Kuru dynasty flourished in the kingdom of Hastinapura. I see the city—its golden palaces gleaming under the sun, its streets alive with the chatter of merchants, the clash of swords in training grounds, and the chants of priests in temples. The Pandavas and Kauravas, cousins destined for rivalry, were young princes training under the renowned guru Dronacharya, a master of warfare whose wisdom and skill were unmatched. I see Dronacharya—his form tall and stern, his eyes sharp with knowledge, his heart devoted to shaping warriors who would uphold dharma. Among his students, Arjuna, the third Pandava, was his favorite, a prodigy whose archery skills dazzled all. I see Arjuna—his youthful face focused, his bow Gandiva already a symbol of his future greatness, his heart burning with ambition to be the greatest archer in the world.

Far from the grandeur of Hastinapura, in a dense forest near the kingdom's borders, lived the Nishada tribe, a community of hunters skilled in the ways of the wild. Among them was a boy named Ekalavya, the son of a tribal chief, whose heart beat with a dream as vast as the sky—to become the greatest archer the world had ever seen. I see Ekalavya—his skin dark as the forest soil, his eyes bright with determination, his body lean and strong from years of hunting with his father. From a young age, Ekalavya had watched birds soar and deer leap, dreaming of arrows that could match their grace and speed. I feel his longing—a boy whose world was the forest, yet whose heart yearned for the glory of a warrior.

Ekalavya's father, Hiranyadhanus, was a skilled hunter but a simple man, content with his tribe's ways. I see Hiranyadhanus—his hands rough from wielding a bow, his smile warm as he taught Ekalavya to track animals. "The forest is our home, son. It gives us all we need," he would say. But Ekalavya's heart was restless. He had heard tales of Dronacharya, the guru who trained princes, whose knowledge could turn a boy into a legend. I feel Ekalavya's resolve—a fire in his chest, a dream that refused to dim. One day, he approached his father, his voice steady but his eyes pleading. "Father, I wish to learn from Dronacharya. I want to be an archer, not just a hunter." Hiranyadhanus hesitated, his heart torn. "The guru teaches princes, not tribal boys," he warned. But seeing Ekalavya's determination, he relented, his love for his son outweighing his fears.

Ekalavya set out for Hastinapura, his heart pounding with hope, his simple bow slung across his shoulder. I see that journey—Ekalavya walking through forests and rivers, his feet bare, his mind fixed on his dream. He reached Dronacharya's ashram, a serene place where the Pandavas and Kauravas trained under the guru's watchful eye. I see the ashram—huts made of mud and straw, a clearing where targets stood, the air filled with the twang of bows and the laughter of young princes. Ekalavya approached Dronacharya, his head bowed in respect, his voice trembling with awe. "Guruji, I am Ekalavya, a Nishada boy. I wish to learn archery from you. Please accept me as your disciple."

Dronacharya looked at the boy, his eyes taking in Ekalavya's humble clothes, his tribal features, his earnest gaze. I feel the guru's conflict—Dronacharya, a man of dharma, bound by the rules of the time. He had vowed to train only the Kuru princes, a promise made to the royal family. The laws of society were strict—tribal boys like Ekalavya were not meant to learn the arts of kshatriyas, the warrior class. "I cannot teach you, child," Dronacharya said, his voice firm but his heart heavy. "I am bound by my duty to the princes of Hastinapura." I see Ekalavya's face—his hope crumbling, his eyes filling with tears, yet his spirit unbroken.

Ekalavya returned to his forest, his dream shattered but not destroyed. I feel his determination—a fire that burned brighter in the face of rejection. If Dronacharya would not teach him, he would find a way to learn. In a clearing deep in the forest, Ekalavya built a clay statue of Dronacharya, crafting it with his own hands, pouring his devotion into every detail. I see that statue—Dronacharya's form, stern yet wise, standing under a peepal tree, a symbol of Ekalavya's unyielding faith. Ekalavya bowed before the statue, declaring, "You are my guru, even if you did not accept me. I will learn from your spirit." I feel his reverence—a boy whose heart saw no difference between a living guru and a clay one, his devotion pure and boundless.

From that day, Ekalavya trained with a discipline that would shame even the greatest warriors. He rose before dawn, his body shivering in the morning mist, and practiced archery until the stars appeared. I see him—Ekalavya, his fingers calloused from drawing his bow, his eyes sharp as he aimed at leaves, birds, and imaginary foes. He learned from the forest—watching how the wind bent the trees, how animals moved, how silence could be a weapon. I feel his growth—a boy becoming a master, his arrows flying faster and truer with each passing day. He meditated before the clay statue, seeking Dronacharya's blessings in his heart, his faith unwavering. I see that scene—Ekalavya, his body glistening with sweat, his mind focused, his arrows piercing targets with a precision that seemed almost divine.

Years passed, and Ekalavya's skill grew to rival even Arjuna's. I feel that parallel—two boys, one a prince and one a tribal, both archers of unparalleled talent, their paths destined to cross. One day, the Pandavas and Kauravas were hunting in the forest near Ekalavya's home, their laughter echoing through the trees. A dog, belonging to the princes, wandered into Ekalavya's clearing, barking loudly and disturbing his practice. I see that moment—Ekalavya, his focus broken, his eyes narrowing as the dog yapped. In a flash, he shot seven arrows, not to harm the dog but to seal its mouth shut without drawing blood, a feat of precision that stunned even the forest spirits. I feel the awe—that dog, its mouth pinned by arrows, running back to the princes, a silent testament to Ekalavya's skill.

The Pandavas and Kauravas were amazed, their hearts filled with wonder and envy. "Who could have done this?" Arjuna asked, his pride as an archer shaken. They followed the dog's trail and found Ekalavya, still practicing before the clay statue of Dronacharya. I see that encounter—Ekalavya, his simple dhoti stained with earth, his bow in hand, his face calm yet proud. "Who are you, and who taught you this skill?" Dronacharya asked, his voice a mix of curiosity and concern. Ekalavya bowed low, his eyes shining with devotion. "I am Ekalavya, a Nishada boy. You are my guru, Guruji. I learned by your blessings, through this statue I made of you." I feel Dronacharya's shock—a guru who had refused a student, now revered in clay, his teachings absorbed through sheer faith.

Arjuna's heart burned with jealousy, his dream of being the greatest archer threatened. I see Arjuna—his face clouded, his voice low as he spoke to Dronacharya. "Guruji, you promised I would be the best archer in the world. How can this boy, a tribal, surpass me?" Dronacharya's heart sank, torn between his love for Arjuna and the injustice of Ekalavya's talent. I feel the guru's dilemma—a man of dharma, bound by a promise, yet moved by Ekalavya's devotion. The laws of the time favored princes over tribals, and Dronacharya knew that Arjuna's role in the coming war for dharma was crucial. But Ekalavya's skill, born of pure dedication, could not be ignored.

Dronacharya approached Ekalavya, his voice heavy with a decision that would haunt him. "If I am your guru, Ekalavya, you owe me guru-dakshina, a gift of gratitude." Ekalavya's eyes lit up, his heart eager to honor his guru. "Anything, Guruji. My life is yours," he said, his voice trembling with loyalty. I feel that moment—Ekalavya, his faith unshaken, ready to give anything for the guru he loved. Dronacharya's next words were like a thunderbolt, shattering the forest's silence. "Give me the thumb of your right hand," he said, his voice steady but his heart breaking. I see Ekalavya's face—shock giving way to understanding, his eyes filling with tears, yet his resolve firm.

The Pandavas and Kauravas gasped, their hearts torn between awe and horror. I feel their conflict—Arjuna, relieved yet ashamed; Bhima, angry at the injustice; Yudhishthira, silent with sorrow. Ekalavya looked at the clay statue, his guru's image, and smiled through his tears. "If this is your wish, Guruji, I will obey," he said. Without hesitation, he took a knife, his hands steady, and severed the thumb of his right hand, the very thumb that drew his bowstring, the key to his archery. I see that sacrifice—blood pooling on the forest floor, Ekalavya's face pale but serene, his thumb offered at Dronacharya's feet. I feel his pain—a boy giving up his dream, his skill, his identity, all for the sake of dharma and loyalty.

Dronacharya's eyes filled with tears, his heart heavy with the weight of Ekalavya's sacrifice. "Your devotion is unmatched, Ekalavya. Your name will live forever," he said, his voice choked with emotion. I see the guru—his hands trembling as he accepted the thumb, his soul burdened by the cost of his demand. Ekalavya smiled, his heart at peace, his loyalty fulfilled. But his archery was crippled, his dream shattered by the very guru he revered. I feel that tragedy—a boy whose talent rivaled the gods, now unable to draw a bow, his sacrifice a testament to dharma's harsh demands.

Ekalavya returned to his tribe, his spirit unbroken, his heart still pure. I see him—Ekalavya, his right hand bandaged, teaching his people with the same dedication, his legacy one of honor, not arrows. In the Mahabharata, Ekalavya's story became a legend, a reminder of the complexities of dharma, the pain of sacrifice, and the power of loyalty. I feel its echo—a tale that challenges the heart, asking what is right, what is fair, and what is the true cost of greatness.

This story is of dedication, sacrifice, and the bittersweet cost of dharma. It teaches that true loyalty can demand the greatest sacrifices, and dharma's path is often paved with pain. Ekalavya's sacrifice and Dronacharya's demand leave a scar on my heart, proclaiming that honor comes at a price, yet shines brighter than any victory.

And so, the story of Ekalavya's Sacrifice, drawn from the Mahabharata, shines with dedication, sacrifice, and the tragic beauty of dharma. It echoes in tales of loyalty, reminding us that greatness often comes with a cost. It teaches that dharma's demands can break the heart, yet honor endures. Ekalavya's sacrifice and Dronacharya's burden inspire us, showing that loyalty is eternal, even in pain. When I see a bow, I feel Ekalavya's thumb, a silent promise of honor's price.

Story 30: Sudama's Friendship with Krishna

The tale of Sudama's Friendship with Krishna melts my heart like a flute's melody, weaving a saga of humility, friendship, and divine love that fills the soul with warmth and wonder. Found in the Bhagavata Purana, this is the story of Sudama, a poor Brahmin whose simple devotion and lifelong friendship with Krishna, the divine king, revealed the boundless love of the divine for a humble heart. Sudama, whose poverty could not dim his faith, and Krishna, whose divinity embraced the simplest offering, are the heart of this tender narrative. This story fills me with joy and reverence, teaching that true friendship transcends wealth, and divine love accepts the humblest gifts with the greatest joy. Let's journey to a time when a poor man's offering shook the heavens, a god's love lit the path to grace, and friendship shone brighter than gold.

In the age of the Dwapara Yuga, when the earth was blessed by the presence of Krishna, the divine incarnation of Vishnu, the city of Dwaraka stood as a jewel by the sea, its golden spires gleaming under the sun. I see Dwaraka—its streets bustling with devotees, its palaces radiant with divine energy, its air filled with the chants of Krishna's name. Krishna, now a king, ruled with love and wisdom, his heart as vast as the ocean, his smile a beacon for all.

I see Krishna—His blue skin glowing, His yellow dhoti shimmering, His flute tucked at His waist, His eyes filled with mischief and mercy. Beside Him was Rukmini, His queen, her grace a perfect match for His divinity. I feel their bond—a love that was both royal and divine, a partnership that blessed Dwaraka.

Far from Dwaraka, in a small village near Mathura, lived Sudama, a poor Brahmin who had once been Krishna's childhood friend. I see Sudama—his body thin from hunger, his clothes patched and faded, his face lined with the struggles of poverty, yet his eyes bright with faith. Sudama and Krishna had studied together at the ashram of Sage Sandipani, their friendship forged in the innocence of youth. I see those days—two boys, one a prince and one a Brahmin, laughing as they gathered firewood, sharing simple meals, their hearts bound by a love that knew no difference of status. Krishna, even then, was divine, His mischief lighting up the ashram, while Sudama, quiet and devout, found joy in His presence. I feel their friendship—a bond so pure, it was like the Ganga's flow, eternal and untainted.

Years had passed since those ashram days, and life had taken the friends on different paths. Krishna became the king of Dwaraka, His divine leelas a legend, while Sudama lived in poverty, his days spent chanting mantras and teaching children for meager alms. I see Sudama's hut—a small, mud-walled home, its roof leaking in the rains, its floor bare but for a straw mat. Sudama's wife, Sushila, was his strength, her love unwavering despite their hardships. I see Sushila—her saree faded, her hands rough from work, her smile gentle as she cared for their two children, a boy and a girl, whose laughter was their only wealth. I feel their struggle—a family bound by love, yet weighed down by want, their meals often just a handful of rice or wild greens.

One evening, as Sudama and Sushila sat outside their hut, the children asleep, Sushila spoke softly, her voice tinged with worry. "Our children go hungry, husband. We have nothing left. Why don't you go to Dwaraka and seek Krishna's help? He was your friend, and they say He is as generous as He is divine." I see Sudama's face—his heart torn, his pride as a Brahmin clashing with his love for his family. "Krishna is a king now, Sushila. I am a poor man. How can I go to Him with empty hands?" he asked, his voice heavy. But Sushila smiled, her faith in Krishna unshaken. "He is your friend, not just a king. Take a small gift, something from our home, and go with love." I feel her hope—a wife who saw beyond poverty, her trust in Krishna a light in their darkness. Sudama nodded, his heart warmed by her words. Sushila gathered a handful of flattened rice, the only food they had, and tied it in a small, tattered cloth. I see that bundle—grains of rice, dry and simple, yet carrying the weight of their love and faith. Sudama set out for Dwaraka the next morning, his bare feet treading the long road, his heart a mix of hope and fear. I see that journey—Sudama walking through dusty paths, past rivers and fields, his body frail but his spirit strong, the bundle of rice clutched in his hand. He chanted Krishna's name with every step, his heart whispering, "Will He remember me? Will He accept my humble gift?" I feel his humility—a man whose love for his friend outweighed his shame, his faith a shield against doubt.

After days of travel, Sudama reached Dwaraka, its grandeur overwhelming his simple heart. I see the city gates—guarded by warriors, adorned with flags, the air filled with the scent of sandalwood and the sound of conches. Sudama hesitated, his tattered clothes a stark contrast to the city's splendor, his bundle of rice feeling smaller in his hands. But he gathered his courage and approached the palace, his heart beating with the hope of seeing Krishna. The guards, seeing his poverty, mocked him, their laughter sharp. "A beggar for the king? Go away!" they sneered. I feel Sudama's pain—his head bowed, his heart aching, yet his faith unshaken.

Krishna, whose divine vision saw all, sensed Sudama's presence, His heart leaping with joy at the thought of His friend. I see Krishna—His eyes lighting up, His voice urgent as He called to His attendants, "Bring him to me at once!" The guards, stunned by Krishna's command, led Sudama into the palace, their mockery silenced. I see that moment—Sudama stepping into the royal court, its marble floors gleaming, its walls adorned with jewels, Rukmini smiling warmly beside Krishna. Sudama's heart raced, his eyes lowering in shame at his appearance, but Krishna ran to him, His arms wide, His laughter like music. "Sudama, my friend!" Krishna cried, embracing him tightly, heedless of Sudama's tattered clothes. I feel that reunion—Krishna, a king, embracing a poor Brahmin, their friendship a bridge over the chasm of status.

Krishna led Sudama to a golden seat, washing his feet with His own hands, a gesture of love that moved the entire court. I see Rukmini—her eyes soft, her hands offering Sudama water and fruits, her heart echoing Krishna's affection. "You've come after so long, my friend. Why didn't you come sooner?" Krishna asked, His voice filled with love. Sudama, overwhelmed, could barely speak, his eyes brimming with tears. "I brought you a small gift, Krishna," he said, his voice trembling as he offered the bundle of flattened rice. I feel his humility—Sudama, his hands shaking, his heart hoping Krishna would accept his simple offering.

Krishna's eyes shone with delight as He took the bundle, unwrapping it with the eagerness of a child. "Flattened rice! My favorite, and from my dearest friend!" He exclaimed, eating a handful with joy, each grain a taste of Sudama's love. I see that moment—Krishna, a king, savoring a poor man's gift, His divine heart melting with gratitude. Rukmini gently stopped Him after the second handful, her smile knowing, for she understood Krishna's divine play. I feel the magic—Krishna's love transforming that rice into a blessing, a gift that would change Sudama's life.

Sudama spent the day with Krishna, their laughter filling the palace as they reminisced about their ashram days—stealing butter, racing through fields, studying under Sandipani's stern gaze. I see their joy—Krishna, His flute forgotten, His heart a boy's again, Sudama, his poverty forgotten, his soul lifted by friendship. When it was time to leave, Sudama felt a pang of guilt—he had not asked for help, his pride as a Brahmin holding him back. Krishna, knowing his heart, smiled, His eyes promising more than words could say. "Take my love back to Sushila and your children," Krishna said, embracing Sudama once more. I feel that farewell—Sudama, his heart full, his bundle empty, yet his soul richer than ever.

Sudama returned to his village, his steps lighter, his heart singing Krishna's name. But when he reached his home, he stood frozen, his eyes wide with wonder. His mud hut was gone, replaced by a grand mansion, its walls adorned with flowers, its courtyard filled with grain and cattle. I see that transformation—Sushila and the children, dressed in fine clothes, running to him, their faces glowing with joy. "Krishna's love has blessed us!" Sushila cried, her eyes shining with gratitude. I feel Sudama's awe—a poor Brahmin, now blessed with wealth, yet his heart unchanged, his devotion to Krishna deeper than ever.

Sudama lived the rest of his days in humility, using his wealth to help others, his heart forever tied to Krishna. I see him—Sudama, chanting Krishna's name, teaching his children the value of friendship, his life a testament to divine love. In the Bhagavata Purana, Sudama's story became a song of devotion, a reminder that the divine accepts the humblest offerings with the greatest love. I feel its warmth—a tale that heals the heart, showing that true friendship and faith can move the gods themselves.

This story is of humility, friendship, and divine love. It teaches that the simplest gifts, given with love, are the most precious to the divine, and true friendship transcends all differences. Sudama's rice and Krishna's love light a lamp in my heart, proclaiming that devotion and friendship are the true treasures of life.

And so, the tale of Sudama's Friendship with Krishna, drawn from the Bhagavata Purana, shines with humility, friendship, and divine love's glory. It echoes in songs of devotion, reminding us that the divine cherishes the heart's offerings. It teaches that friendship and faith conquer all barriers. Sudama's rice and Krishna's grace inspire us, showing that love is eternal, even in the humblest forms. When I hear a flute, I feel Sudama's joy, promising friendship's divine light.

Story 31: The Call to Lanka

Let me take you back to a time when the world was filled with devotion, valor, and divine mysteries. A time when Lord Rama, the seventh incarnation of Lord Vishnu, walked the earth, and his devoted follower, Hanuman, the monkey god, became the symbol of strength, loyalty, and courage. This is the story of Hanuman's first journey to Lanka, a tale that resonates in the hearts of millions, drawn from the sacred pages of the Ramayana and the vibrant oral traditions of Hindu culture. It's a story of faith, trials, and divine intervention, and I'm thrilled to share it with you, as if I'm sitting by a fire under a starry sky, recounting this epic adventure.

The story begins in the lush forests of Kishkindha, where Lord Rama, his brother Lakshmana, and their loyal ally Sugriva, the king of the Vanaras (monkey warriors), were gripped with worry. Mata Sita, Rama's beloved wife, had been abducted by Ravana, the mighty demon king of Lanka. Ravana, with his ten heads and unmatched power, had whisked Sita away to his golden city across the ocean, leaving Rama heartbroken and determined to rescue her.

Rama and Lakshmana had formed an alliance with Sugriva, who promised to help find Sita. The Vanaras were sent in all directions—north, east, west, and south—to search for her. The southern expedition, led by Angada, Sugriva's nephew, included some of the mightiest Vanara warriors, but none shone brighter than Hanuman, the son of Vayu, the wind god. Hanuman was no ordinary being. Born to Anjana and blessed by the gods, he was endowed with immense strength, wisdom, and devotion to Rama. His heart burned with love for his lord, and he was ready to cross any obstacle to serve him.

Weeks passed, and the Vanaras searched tirelessly, combing through forests, mountains, and rivers. They followed every lead, but Sita's whereabouts remained a mystery. As the southern group reached the edge of the land, where the vast ocean stretched endlessly before them, despair set in. The deadline Sugriva had given them was nearing, and they had no clue where Sita was. The Vanaras sat on the sandy shore, their heads bowed, feeling the weight of failure. Angada, their leader, spoke with a heavy heart, "We've searched everywhere, but the trail ends here. How can we face Rama without news of Sita?"

That's when Hanuman, the ever-optimistic and devoted warrior, stood up. His eyes sparkled with determination, and his voice carried the strength of the wind itself. "Friends," he said, "we cannot give up. Lord Rama has placed his trust in us, and I will not let him down. The ocean may seem vast, but I believe Sita is in Lanka, Ravana's kingdom. I will cross this ocean and find her."

The Vanaras looked at Hanuman, their spirits lifting. They knew of his extraordinary powers, but crossing an ocean? That was no small feat. Yet, Hanuman's confidence was infectious. He reminded them of his divine origins and the boons he had received from the gods. As a child, Hanuman had once leapt toward the sun, mistaking it for a ripe fruit, only to be struck down by Indra's thunderbolt. The gods, moved by his innocence, had showered him with blessings—immortality, strength, and the ability to change his size and form at will. Hanuman was no ordinary monkey; he was a divine force.

Before embarking on his journey, Hanuman sought the blessings of his companions and, most importantly, Lord Rama. Rama had given Hanuman his ring as a token for Sita, a symbol that would assure her of Hanuman's authenticity. As Hanuman held the ring, he felt Rama's love and trust flow through him. He closed his eyes and chanted, "Jai Shri Ram!"—a mantra that would guide him through every trial.

Hanuman stood on the Mahendra Mountain, a towering peak overlooking the ocean. The Vanaras gathered around, chanting his name, their voices echoing like a divine chorus. Hanuman invoked the blessings of his father, Vayu, and the gods who had shaped his destiny. He meditated on Rama, visualizing Sita's face, and felt a surge of energy within him. This was no ordinary journey; it was a sacred mission, a test of his devotion and strength.

Now, let me pause here to share a beautiful belief tied to this moment. In many parts of India, devotees chant the *Hanuman Chalisa*, a 40-verse hymn composed by Tulsidas, to invoke Hanuman's strength and courage. It's said that reciting the Chalisa with a pure heart can remove obstacles and grant protection, just as Hanuman overcame every challenge in his path. In temples, especially on Tuesdays and Saturdays—days considered auspicious for Hanuman worship—devotees offer sindoor (vermilion) to Hanuman idols, a practice rooted in a legend. It's believed that Hanuman once saw Sita applying sindoor on her forehead and asked why. Sita explained it was for Rama's long life. In his boundless devotion, Hanuman covered his entire body with sindoor to show his love for Rama, which is why Hanuman idols are often smeared with sindoor and oil.

Back to the story—Hanuman took a deep breath, and his body began to grow. The Vanaras watched in awe as he expanded, his form becoming as massive as a mountain, his muscles rippling with divine energy. His tail curled high, and his eyes glowed with resolve. With a mighty roar of "Jai Shri Ram!" he leapt into the sky, soaring over the ocean like a comet. The wind, his father Vayu, carried him forward, and the gods themselves watched in wonder.

The First Challenge: Mainaka, the Golden Mountain

As Hanuman flew over the ocean, the waves below roared, and the wind howled around him. His journey had just begun, but the first test was already approaching. Deep beneath the ocean, a golden mountain named Mainaka, son of Himavan (the mountain king) and Menaka, rose to meet him. Mainaka was no ordinary mountain. In ancient times, mountains had wings and could fly, causing chaos by crashing into each other. Indra, the king of gods, had clipped their wings, but Mainaka had escaped by hiding in the ocean, protected by the sea god Varuna.

Mainaka, grateful to Vayu for once saving him from Indra's wrath, wanted to honor Hanuman, Vayu's son. The golden mountain emerged from the waves, its peaks shimmering in the sunlight, and spoke to Hanuman in a gentle, rumbling voice. "O mighty Hanuman, you are on a divine mission. Rest on my peaks for a while, regain your strength, and continue your journey."

Hanuman, however, was focused. His heart was set on Sita, and every moment mattered. He smiled at Mainaka and said, "O noble mountain, I am touched by your kindness, but I cannot stop. My lord Rama awaits news of Sita, and I must not delay." With a respectful touch of his hand on Mainaka's peak, Hanuman soared higher, leaving the mountain in awe of his determination.

This encounter with Mainaka is celebrated in Hindu tradition as a symbol of Hanuman's single-minded devotion. In some regions, devotees tell this story to teach children the value of staying focused on their goals, no matter how tempting distractions may be. Mainaka's offer wasn't a test of malice but a gesture of goodwill, yet Hanuman's refusal shows his unwavering commitment. In rituals, devotees often fast or undertake vows (vrat) in Hanuman's name, seeking his discipline and focus. For example, the *Hanuman Vrat* involves fasting on Tuesdays, chanting the Hanuman Chalisa, and offering bananas or laddoos to Hanuman's idol, believing it brings clarity and strength.

The Second Challenge: Surasa, the Serpent Mother

Hanuman's journey was far from over, and the gods, curious about his prowess, decided to test him further. As he flew through the sky, a massive figure emerged from the ocean—a serpent goddess named Surasa, sent by the gods to challenge Hanuman's wit and power. Surasa was no ordinary being; she was the mother of serpents, a divine entity with a gaping mouth that could swallow mountains. Her eyes gleamed with mischief as she spoke, "O Hanuman, the gods have sent me to test you. You cannot pass unless you enter my mouth."

Hanuman, ever respectful, bowed to Surasa and said, "O divine mother, I am on a sacred mission to find Mata Sita. Allow me to pass, and I will return to fulfill your challenge." But Surasa was firm. "Enter my mouth, or you shall not proceed," she declared, opening her jaws wide enough to block the sky.

Now, Hanuman was no stranger to challenges. He knew brute strength alone wouldn't suffice; he needed cunning. With a twinkle in his eye, he began to grow, his body expanding until he towered over Surasa like a colossal mountain. The serpent goddess, undeterred, stretched her mouth even wider. Hanuman grew larger still, his form blotting out the sun. But then, in a flash of brilliance, he did the unexpected—he shrank to the size of a thumb and darted into Surasa's mouth, zipping out before she could close it.

Surasa laughed, delighted by Hanuman's cleverness. "You have passed my test, O son of Vayu!" she said, blessing him. "Go forth with my blessings, for your wisdom and strength are unmatched." Hanuman bowed humbly and continued his journey, his heart light with the victory.

This story of Surasa is a favorite among devotees, symbolizing Hanuman's ability to adapt and use intelligence over force. In many Hanuman temples, especially in South India, priests recount this tale during festivals like Hanuman Jayanti (celebrated on the full moon day of Chaitra month, usually April). Devotees offer betel leaves and garlands to Hanuman idols, believing it invokes his quick thinking. There's also a folk belief that chanting Hanuman's name during difficult exams or intellectual challenges can sharpen the mind, inspired by his outwitting of Surasa.

The wind roared in my ears as I imagined Hanuman soaring through the sky, his heart pounding with devotion to Lord Rama. The ocean below churned with waves, as if cheering him on, while the stars above twinkled like divine witnesses to his sacred mission. Hanuman had already overcome two challenges—Mainaka, the golden mountain who offered rest, and Surasa, the serpent goddess who tested his wit. But the path to Lanka was not yet clear. The gods, demons, and forces of nature had more in store for the mighty son of Vayu. This is the story of how Hanuman faced the shadow-catching demoness Simhika, entered the fortress of Lanka, and began his search for Mata Sita, all while carrying Rama's love in his heart.

The Third Challenge: Simhika, the Shadow-Catcher

As Hanuman flew over the vast ocean, his body cutting through the clouds like an arrow, a strange sensation gripped him. His speed slowed, as if an invisible force was pulling him back. He looked around, his sharp eyes scanning the horizon, but saw nothing but waves and sky. Then, from the depths of the ocean, a dark shadow rose—a monstrous creature named Simhika, a demoness with a terrifying power. Simhika had the ability to seize the shadow of any being flying above her and drag them into her jaws. Her hunger was insatiable, and she had spotted Hanuman, a prize unlike any other.

The ocean churned violently as Simhika emerged, her form grotesque and massive, her eyes glowing with malice. "Who dares cross my waters?" she roared, her voice echoing like thunder. "You, monkey, will be my meal!" Hanuman felt her power tugging at his shadow, slowing his flight. His heart, however, remained steady. He chanted "Jai Shri Ram!" under his breath, drawing strength from his lord's name.

Hanuman knew this was no ordinary foe. Simhika's power lay in her ability to trap him through his shadow, a mystical force tied to his very being. But Hanuman was no stranger to divine tricks. He remembered the blessings of the gods—his ability to change size and form at will. With a mischievous grin, he began to grow, his body expanding until he loomed like a mountain in the sky. Simhika, undeterred, stretched her jaws wider, her shadowy grip tightening.

But Hanuman was clever. Just as he had outwitted Surasa, he now shrank in an instant, becoming smaller than a sparrow. Before Simhika could react, he dove into her open mouth, flew through her body, and struck her vital organs with his mighty fists. The demoness let out a piercing scream, her form collapsing into the ocean as her shadow-catching power faded. Hanuman emerged unharmed, his heart pounding with triumph. The gods, watching from the heavens, applauded his strength and cunning. This encounter with Simhika is one of the most thrilling episodes in Hanuman's journey, symbolizing his ability to overcome even the most insidious obstacles. In Hindu tradition, Simhika represents the hidden fears and doubts that lurk in the shadows of our minds. Devotees often tell this story to teach that chanting Hanuman's name can dispel negative energies, much like Hanuman destroyed Simhika. In many Hanuman temples, especially in North India, priests light ghee lamps before Hanuman idols to ward off "evil shadows" or negative influences. This ritual, called *deep daan*, involves offering a lamp with five wicks, symbolizing the five elements, and is believed to invoke Hanuman's protection.

There's also a folk belief tied to this story. In some villages, people tie black threads blessed at Hanuman temples around their wrists or ankles to protect against "nazar" (evil eye) or negative energies, inspired by Hanuman's victory over Simhika's shadowy grasp. During Hanuman Jayanti celebrations, devotees sing bhajans recounting this tale, their voices rising in praise of Hanuman's courage. The line from the *Hanuman Chalisa*—"Sankat te Hanuman chhudave" (Hanuman delivers us from danger)—is often chanted with extra fervor, as it's believed to echo his triumph over Simhika.

Arrival in Lanka: The Golden City

With Simhika defeated, Hanuman's path was clear. The ocean stretched endlessly before him, but his heart was light, fueled by his devotion to Rama. As the sun began to set, painting the sky in hues of orange and gold, Hanuman spotted a shimmering island in the distance—Lanka, the golden city of Ravana. Its towers gleamed like fire, its walls fortified with magic and might. This was no ordinary place; it was the stronghold of the demon king, protected by divine and demonic forces alike.

Hanuman slowed his flight, his mind racing. Lanka was a fortress unlike any other, guarded by Ravana's army and mystical powers. He knew he couldn't enter as a towering giant; stealth was his ally now. Shrinking to the size of a cat, Hanuman landed softly on the shores of Lanka, his eyes wide with wonder and caution. The city was a marvel—palaces of gold, gardens blooming with exotic flowers, and streets bustling with Rakshasas (demons) who served Ravana. Yet, beneath its beauty lay a sense of oppression, as if the city itself knew of Ravana's sin in abducting Sita.

Before Hanuman could take another step, a powerful presence blocked his path. It was Lankini, the guardian goddess of Lanka, a fierce deity appointed by Brahma to protect the city. Lankini was no ordinary guard; she was a divine being with immense strength, her form towering and radiant, yet her eyes burned with a challenge. "Who are you, little monkey, daring to enter

Ravana's city?" she demanded, her voice shaking the ground. "No one enters Lanka without my permission!"

Hanuman, ever humble, bowed respectfully. "O great goddess, I am Hanuman, a servant of Lord Rama. I come in search of Mata Sita, who was unjustly taken by your king. Let me pass, for my mission is pure." Lankini, bound by her duty, laughed. "A mere monkey challenges me? Turn back, or face my wrath!"

Hanuman knew he couldn't avoid this test. With a prayer to Rama, he prepared for battle. Lankini swung her massive arm, but Hanuman was swift. He dodged her blow and, with a single strike of his fist—gentle yet powerful—knocked her to the ground. Lankini, stunned, rose slowly, her pride humbled. But instead of anger, her face softened. She recognized Hanuman's divine aura and remembered a prophecy: "When a monkey defeats you, Lankini, know that Ravana's end is near."

"O Hanuman," she said, her voice trembling with awe, "you are no ordinary being. Go, find Sita, and fulfill your mission. My blessings are with you." With that, Lankini stepped aside, allowing Hanuman to enter Lanka. This moment is etched in the Ramayana as a turning point, signaling the beginning of Ravana's downfall.

The story of Lankini is deeply revered in Hindu tradition. It's said that her defeat by Hanuman symbolizes the triumph of righteousness over pride. In some South Indian temples, especially in Tamil Nadu, devotees offer coconuts to Hanuman idols, breaking them as a symbol of breaking ego and obstacles, inspired by Hanuman's humbling of Lankini. The coconut ritual, called *nariyal chadhana*, is believed to clear the path for success, much like Hanuman cleared his path into Lanka. In rural areas, storytellers often describe Lankini as a reminder that even divine beings bow to true devotion, and devotees are encouraged to approach Hanuman with humility.

Exploring Lanka: A City of Splendor and Sin

With Lankini's blessing, Hanuman slipped into Lanka, his tiny form moving like a shadow through the city's golden streets. The sights overwhelmed him—palaces adorned with jewels, fountains sparkling under the moonlight, and Rakshasas reveling in Ravana's wealth. Yet, Hanuman's heart was heavy. Somewhere in this opulent prison, Sita was suffering, separated from Rama. He vowed to find her, no matter the cost.

Hanuman leapt from rooftop to rooftop, his eyes scanning every corner. He entered Ravana's grand palace, its halls filled with treasures and guarded by fierce Rakshasas. He saw Ravana himself, sleeping on a golden bed, surrounded by his queens. But Sita was nowhere to be found. Hanuman's heart sank—had he come so far only to fail? Yet, he remembered Rama's words: "Find her, Hanuman. She is my life." With renewed resolve, he continued his search, moving silently through the city.

As he explored, Hanuman faced no physical foes, but the city itself was a temptation. Lanka's beauty could sway even the strongest heart, whispering promises of luxury and power. But Hanuman was unshakable. His devotion to Rama was his shield, and every step he took was a prayer. Finally, he reached a grove unlike any other—a garden of Ashoka trees, their red blossoms glowing under the moon. This was the Ashoka Vatika, a place of both beauty and sorrow.

Let me share a beautiful tradition tied to this moment. The Ashoka tree, meaning "without sorrow," is sacred in Hinduism, believed to bring peace and remove grief. Devotees plant Ashoka trees near Hanuman temples, and during festivals, they offer its leaves in puja, seeking relief from worries. The Ashoka Vatika, where Hanuman would soon find Sita, is seen as a symbol of hope amidst despair. In many homes, women tie threads around Ashoka trees or place Hanuman idols beneath them, praying for strength and protection, inspired by Hanuman's journey.

Cultural and Spiritual Significance

Hanuman's encounters with Simhika and Lankini, and his stealthy exploration of Lanka, are more than just thrilling tales—they're lessons in courage, humility, and focus. Simhika's shadow represents the unseen fears that hold us back, while Lankini's defeat shows that even the mightiest obstacles yield to devotion. Hanuman's ability to navigate Lanka's temptations teaches us to stay true to our purpose, no matter how dazzling the distractions.

In devotional practices, these stories inspire countless rituals. During Hanuman Jayanti, celebrated with fervor across India, devotees visit temples like the Sankat Mochan in Varanasi or the Hanuman Garhi in Ayodhya, offering sindoor, oil, and sweets like laddoos. The *Hanuman Ashtak*, a prayer praising Hanuman's eight great deeds, is chanted to invoke his protection, with verses often referencing his Lanka journey. In some regions, especially in Maharashtra, devotees perform *Hanuman Kavach* recitations, a protective hymn believed to shield against evil forces, drawing from Hanuman's victory over Simhika.

There's also a charming legend about Hanuman's shadow. Some believe that Hanuman's shadow, freed from Simhika's grasp, became a symbol of his elusive power. In certain temples, priests draw Hanuman's silhouette on walls during rituals, believing it carries his protective energy. Devotees touch these drawings, seeking blessings for safety on their own journeys.

Conclusion: A Tapestry of Eternal Truths

As I sit here, penning the final words of this book, my heart feels like a river swollen with the stories we've shared, each tale a shimmering wave carrying devotion, courage, sacrifice, and wisdom. These 28 stories, drawn from the sacred wells of the Hindu Puranas, Mahabharata, Ramayana, and Upanishads, have been my companions, my teachers, and my solace. They've taken us on a journey through divine realms and human hearts, from the cosmic churn of the ocean to the quiet curiosity of a boy facing death. Together, we've sat by an imaginary fire under a banyan tree, its branches heavy with the weight of ancient truths, its leaves whispering tales that make the soul tremble and soar. This book is more than a collection of stories—it's a pilgrimage, a mirror, and a lamp, guiding us through the eternal dance of dharma, love, and divine grace.

The stories we've explored—each a jewel in its own right—form a tapestry that stretches across time, weaving together the divine and the mortal, the epic and the intimate. From the **Ocean Churning**, where gods and demons united to seek immortality, to **Nachiketa's bold dialogue with Yama**, where a boy uncovered the soul's eternity, these narratives have shown us the vastness of creation and the depth of the human spirit. They've carried us through moments of triumph and tragedy, from **Durga's victory**

over Mahishasura to **Harishchandra's heart-wrenching sacrifice for truth**, from **Rama and Sita's exile** to **Yayati's restless chase for youth** and **Ekalavya's Sacrifice, Sudama's Friendship with Krishna**. Each tale, crafted with care, has poured vivid colors onto the canvas of our imagination—lush forests, radiant deities, thundering battles, and silent prayers.

The Threads That Bind

What binds these stories, so diverse in scope and setting, is their shared heartbeat—dharma, the eternal law that upholds creation. Dharma pulses through every tale, whether it's Rama's duty to his father, Harishchandra's vow of truth, or Arjuna's fight for justice. These stories show dharma's many faces—devotion in Prahlada, compassion in Shibi, wisdom in Nachiketa, and love in Savitri. They remind us that dharma isn't a rigid code but a living force, guiding us through life's joys and sorrows.

Another thread is devotion, the soul's cry to the divine. From Gajendra's desperate prayer to Parvati's penance for Shiva, devotion bridges the mortal and divine. I see these moments—Prahlada chanting Vishnu's name, Markandeya embracing the linga, Bhagiratha standing in penance for Ganga. Devotion, these stories teach, is a fire that burns away fear, doubt, and ego, drawing the divine closer. It's not blind faith but a conscious choice, a surrender that empowers, as Gajendra's lotus and Nachiketa's questions show.

Sacrifice weaves through every tale, a testament to love and duty. Harishchandra gave his kingdom, Shibi his flesh, Savitri her comfort, and Yayati his youth's illusion. I feel their pain—Harishchandra's heart breaking as he sold his family, Shibi's blood pooling for a dove, Savitri's feet bleeding on her quest. Sacrifice, these stories whisper, is the price of dharma, but it's also its reward, bringing divine grace, as Vishnu's chakra, Shiva's boon, or Yama's wisdom prove.

Courage, too, shines brightly—Arjuna facing Shiva's test, Durga battling Mahishasura, Nachiketa confronting death. I see their resolve—Arjuna's arrows flying, Durga's spear gleaming, Nachiketa's voice steady before Yama. Courage isn't just physical; it's the heart's strength to choose truth, as Harishchandra did, or to forgive, as Ahalya's redemption shows. These stories teach that courage, rooted in dharma, transforms trials into triumphs.

Wisdom, the final thread, illuminates these tales like a lamp in darkness. Nachiketa's quest for truth, Yayati's realization of desire's futility, and Krishna's guidance to Arjuna reveal wisdom's power to guide. I hear their voices—Yama's teachings on the Atman, Yayati's weary sigh, Krishna's flute weaving divine counsel. Wisdom, these stories affirm, is not mere knowledge but understanding life's impermanence and the soul's eternity.

Timeless Relevance

Why do these ancient stories matter today, in a world of

smartphones and skyscrapers? Because they speak to the heart's eternal questions—who are we, why do we suffer, what is our purpose? In a world chasing fleeting pleasures, Yayati's tale warns us of desire's emptiness. In times of injustice, Arjuna's quest inspires us to arm ourselves with courage and skill. When despair grips us, Gajendra's prayer reminds us that divine help is a heartbeat away.

These stories offer solace in grief, as Savitri's love defies death, and hope in darkness, as Deepavali's lamps echo Narakasura's defeat. They teach forgiveness through Ahalya, resilience through Harishchandra, and humility through Vamana. In a divided world, Mohini's unity of gods and demons, and Shibi's mercy for a dove, urge us to see divinity in all. Nachiketa's dialogue with Yama speaks to our fear of mortality, assuring us the soul is eternal, a truth science cannot touch but the heart knows.

They also connect us to our roots, a cultural heritage that spans millennia. The Ganga of Bhagiratha flows in India's rivers, Shiva's dance in temple sculptures, Krishna's flute in festival songs. These stories are not relics but living traditions, sung in bhajans, enacted in Ramlilas, and whispered in prayers. They remind us of India's spiritual wealth, a legacy that transcends borders, inviting all to drink from its wisdom.

A Personal Reflection

Writing these stories has been a pilgrimage for me, each word a step toward the divine. I've wept with Harishchandra's loss, danced with Krishna's gopis, trembled with Arjuna's bow, and stood in awe with Nachiketa's truth. These tales have been my mirror, showing my own desires, fears, and hopes. Yayati's chase for youth reflected my own restless moments; Gajendra's surrender taught me to trust in crises; Shibi's compassion urged me to give without counting the cost.

I've felt the gods' presence—Vishnu's chakra flashing, Shiva's trident gleaming, Durga's roar shaking my soul. Yet, these stories also showed the divine in humans—Rama's sacrifice, Draupadi's fire, Parvati's love. They've taught me that divinity isn't distant but within, in every act of kindness, every moment of truth, every prayer of faith.

Sharing these stories with you, dear reader, has been like lighting a lamp in a temple, hoping its glow reaches your heart. I imagine us by that banyan tree, the fire crackling, the night alive with stars, as I recount Rama's exile or Mohini's dance. Your journey through these pages—laughing, weeping, wondering—has made these tales live again, a sacred bond between us.

An Invitation to Live the Stories

As you close this book, I invite you to carry these stories into your life. Let Harishchandra's truth guide your words, Shibi's compassion shape your actions, and Nachiketa's curiosity fuel your questions. When life tests you, remember Arjuna's resolve,

Savitri's love, and Gajendra's faith. When joy fills you, dance like Krishna, love like Parvati, and celebrate like Deepavali's lamps.

These stories aren't just to read but to live. Light a lamp for Durga's strength, offer a lotus for Gajendra's surrender, or chant Shiva's name like Markandeya. Share these tales with children, so Ganesha's wisdom and Rama's duty inspire them. In moments of doubt, hear Vishnu's conch, Krishna's flute, or Yama's wisdom, guiding you to dharma.

The Puranas and epics are an ocean, and we've touched but a few waves. Tales like Ekalavya's sacrifice, Sudama's friendship, or Karna's tragedy await, each a pearl of truth. But these 28 stories are enough to light your path, a constellation of dharma, devotion, and love. They remind us that life is a leela, a divine play, where every struggle leads to grace, every question to truth.

A Final Prayer

As I end, I offer a prayer, like Gajendra's lotus or Nachiketa's boon. May Vishnu's chakra guard you, Shiva's trident empower you, and Durga's spear vanquish your fears. May Krishna's flute bring joy, Rama's bow bring justice, and Parvati's love bring peace. May you walk with Harishchandra's truth, Shibi's mercy, and Arjuna's courage, your soul as eternal as Nachiketa's Atman. Thank you for joining me under this banyan tree, for listening as I poured my heart into these tales. May these stories be your lamp in darkness, your strength in trials, and your song in joy. As the fire fades and the stars shine, I leave you with Krishna's smile,

Shiva's blessing, and the Puranas' eternal whisper—dharma triumphs, love endures, and the soul is forever free.

- RAJNISH KUMAR

https://sanskarsarovar.blogspot.com/

puruji.rk@gmail.com

+91-9855103353

ॐ शान्तिः शान्तिः शान्तिः॥

Om Shāntih Shāntih Shāntih

May peace prevail in the body, mind, and soul.
May the stories stay with you, lighting your path ahead.